Light It Up Red

Vancouver Knights
Book 3

kylie Kent

ISBN 13: 978-1-923137-03-5 (ebook)
978-1-923137-33-2(paperback)

Editing by - Kat Pagan

Club Omerta

Are you a part of the Club?

Don't want to wait for the next book to be released to the public?
Come and Club Omerta for an all access pass!

This includes:
• daily chapter reveals,
• first to see - everything, covers, teasers, blurbs
• Advanced reader copies of every book
• Bonus scenes from the characters you love!
• and so much more

Click the link to be inducted to the club!!!
CLUB OMERTA

Prologue

Liliana

The phone drops with a loud clatter. Shot. He's been shot. My blood is cold. Everything is cold as I hit the hard tiles of the kitchen floor.

No. I shake my head. *This is not happening.*

He's a hockey player. Sure, it's not the safest job

in the world. But when you compare it to what my family does for a living, well, it's pretty damn safe.

This isn't supposed to happen. This shouldn't be happening.

"Lil, shit, what's wrong?" My mom's voice has me looking up. She reaches out and moves my hands away from my hair. I didn't realize I was pulling at it until she pries my fingers from the roots. "Lil, what's wrong?" she asks again, her voice rushed. Panicked.

I peer up at her with tears running down my face. "He got shot."

"Who?"

"Travis... he's..." I can't even finish the sentence. That's when the anger starts to take over, quickly replacing the shock. I push myself up to my feet. "He did it. He actually did it," I hiss as I move to step around my mother.

"What? Who?" The sound of her footsteps follow me down the hall. I don't stop or bother to answer her.

I pick up my pace as I storm towards my father's office. I always thought his threats were just that. *Threats*. I never, in a million years, would have thought he'd follow through with them. I should have known better. My father is the Don of the Valentino

Crime Family. Of course, he means what he says. Of course, his threats aren't empty.

We were raised to believe family above all else. Well, where's that loyalty now?

The two soldiers standing guard at his office door take one look at me and wisely step aside. The door slams against the wall as I shove it open. "I can't believe you!"

My father drops his pistol back onto his desk when his eyes connect with mine, his face twisted with shock. Surprise. I can feel my mom's hands gripping my arm.

"Liliana, you need to calm down," she says.

"Calm down?" I shake out of her hold and return my focus to my father. "Why? Just tell me why?"

"You need to be more specific, Liliana," he says, his voice calm and his expression devoid of emotion now. Stoic. The way he's mastered it to be.

"Why did you have my boyfriend shot?" I ask him.

"What are you talking about?"

"Travis, he was shot. Who else but you would have a reason to shoot him, Dad?" I yell.

"I didn't do it, Liliana. I don't know what's going on, but I will find out," he says.

"Don't bother. Stay out of it. Stay out of my

business. But be warned... if I find out you had anything to do with this, I will never forgive you." Fresh tears stream down my cheeks as I spit the words.

The hurt I see in my father's eyes doesn't help. He walks around the desk, approaching me like I'm a wounded animal. And I guess, right now, I kind of am.

I hold up a hand to stop him before he reaches me. "Do not touch me."

Then I turn around and run from the office and straight up to my room. I need to find my passport. I need to get on the next flight to Vancouver. Or, better yet, I need the family jet. I pick up my phone and message Alessandro. If anyone can get me on that jet without my father finding out before it takes off, it's my brother.

ME:

> I need you to arrange to have the jet take me to Vancouver. Now.

ALESSANDRO:

> Why?

ME:

> I need to get to Vancouver now. Travis was shot outside the arena. Don't tell Dad I'm going.

ALESSANDRO:

On it, sis.

I toss my phone down on the bed. The door to my room opens and I turn around to find my mother watching me.

"It wasn't him, Lil. Your father would never do anything to hurt you," she says.

"He'd do anything to make sure I never left this house. Let's not pretend otherwise," I counter.

"He wouldn't do *this*," she says more adamantly.

I want to believe her. It would break my heart if my family were the ones behind this. I want to believe that they would never do something so awful to me, but how can I be sure? I was raised to always question every situation. To never fully trust what anyone tells me. But what if the monster I was always supposed to be wary of... is the same one who gave me life?

I'm not stupid. I've heard the horror stories. I've seen how terrified people are of my father. You don't become a Don of a crime family without being ruthless. I've never experienced that side of him, though. He was always just *Dad* to me.

The man who would dance with me for hours on end when I was little, the one who would let me

5

follow him around, even when I knew he was busy. The man who stayed up all night with me, held me in his arms the first time I had my heart broken. He might have been promising to murder the boy who did it, but he was still there for me.

He's always been there for me. My number one supporter. His love for me isn't something I've ever questioned. After all, they say a parent's love knows no bounds. But they say a lot of shit. And not all of it is true.

I told my parents that I was planning to move to Vancouver with Travis last week. And my father had a massive tantrum, forbidding me from leaving the estate. Like I knew he would. He claimed that he couldn't cope with me being in a different house, let alone a different country.

So, I find it hard to believe he didn't have anything to do with Travis being shot a few days later. It can't be a coincidence. Us Valentinos don't believe in coincidences.

Chapter One

Eight months earlier

I cannot believe I let my friends drag me to a sports event. One where I'm literally freezing my ass off at that. Who in their right mind wants to sit in an arena that's set to the same temperature as my refrigerator and watch a bunch of guys skate around and hit something with a stick?

I could think of a lot better ways to spend my Friday night. But the thing about friendships is sometimes you have to take one for the team. My friend Harper is a physical therapist for the NY Strikers. The girl lives for hockey. Personally, I've never seen the appeal.

Did I mention it's cold in here?

I've lived in New York my entire life. I'm used to the season changing, the harsh winters, but this is different. It's a different kind of cold. As I sit here waiting for the players to come out and start doing whatever it is they do.

Harper is buzzing with excitement next to me. "Can you believe these seats? Aren't they amazing?" she screams right into my ear.

"You know my family has a box, right? We could be sitting up there, with the warmth," I tell her while eyeing the expanse of glass windows that overlook the rink.

"But that's not the same experience as being right here. Wait till the game starts. You'll see." She jumps up and down in her seat.

"You do realize that if my cousins are in attendance tonight and they see me down here, they're going to be dragging both of us up to that box."

"Is it dragging if I go willingly?" Harper grins. "I mean, I wouldn't say no to Enzo dragging me off pretty much anywhere."

"Ew, gross. And that's not happening. Trust me when I say you do not want one of my alpha, *I am man* cousins chasing you down."

"What about your brother? He's younger but I could make it work." She laughs.

"Not happening." I shudder at the thought of one of my best friends and Alessandro hooking up.

Just. No.

The announcer starts talking about the teams, and then everyone is suddenly on their feet. Harper yanks at my arm to get me up. I look at her like she's grown two heads. She's jumping around, screaming, and yelling out some nonsense about the Strikers.

I watch as a bunch of players come out onto the ice. They skate across the rink, shooting pucks in every direction. "What are they doing?" I ask her.

"Didn't you just tell me your family had a box?"

"Yeah, and?"

"You've been here before, right? You *have* watched a hockey game before, haven't you?"

"I've never been here, and whenever I've been

forced to watch anything sports related, I usually ignore the world around me and scroll on my socials." I shrug.

"This is just their warm-up. They'll do their stretches and shit before the game actually begins."

"Okay, so why is everyone cheering like they just won a gold medal?" I question her.

"It's the Stanley Cup. They play for the Cup, not a gold medal. And we're cheering because we're supportive of our home team. Like you should be," Harper explains while keeping her eyes on the ice.

"Right, got ya," I grumble under my breath. Which I can see, mind you. I wonder if heated seats are a thing here? If not, they should be.

"I can't believe you're sitting next to me in purple right now," Harper says.

"What's wrong with purple?" I narrow my glare at her. "And this is Chanel," I point out while running a hand down my coat.

"I'm sure it is, but purple is the opposing team's color." She shakes her head at me.

I sit back down and pull my phone out of my bag. There's only so long a girl can watch a guy skate around on ice and hit something with a stick into a net. My eyes are glued to my screen until a knock on the window in front of me has me glancing up. A player in a red and white uniform smiles in my direction. The sharpest blue eyes sear through me and then he turns around and skates off.

The spectators behind me are in an uproar over the interaction. Cheering and chanting a name I can't quite make out. "Who was that?" I ask Harper.

"That was Travis fucking O'Neil. The fact you even have to ask that is just..." She shakes her head again, her expression incredulous. "I clearly have a lot to teach you."

The players all leave the ice again, and I tug on Harper's arm. "Where are they going? Is it over?"

"No, it's not over." She laughs. "It's barely started. They're going to the locker room. They'll be back out." Harper finally sits down and checks her phone. Her lips part on a loud gasp, and her eyes bug out of her head.

"What's wrong?" I ask, peering over while trying to get a look at her screen.

Harper moves her phone out of my sight line. "Come on, I have to go and see one of the players about something," she says.

"You're not working tonight," I remind her.

"I'm always working. If they call, I have to see what they need. It'll only take a sec." She yanks at my hand until I'm standing.

"I can just wait here for you," I suggest.

"And risk you going home? Not a chance. You're watching the whole game and you're watching them win," she says with a definitive nod.

I don't have a choice but to follow Harper when she starts pulling me across the stands. She stops at a gate and shows a security guy her pass. He waves us through and then we're moving down a mirrored tunnel.

But none of this prepares me for the scene we walk into. I stop in my tracks, forcing Harper to pause in front of me. "What?" she asks.

"Harper, this is their dressing room," I whisper. I can feel everyone's eyes on me. All probably wondering what this strange woman is doing in a men's locker room.

"I know. It's awesome, right?" Harper smiles and then continues to drag me along. She comes to a full stop in front of that same player at the window. The one with the blue eyes. "Hey, Travis, what do you need?"

Travis. I roll the name over my tongue. He looks from Harper to me. "Your friend," he says, staring in my direction.

"Excuse me?" I ask, shockingly aware that I'm in the team dressing room all over again.

"You're wearing the wrong color, babe." He reaches behind his back, pulls something out of his bag, and hands it to me. "Put this on. It's a spare."

I look down at his hand and the jersey clutched in his fist. "Why?" I ask him. I happen to really like my purple coat. It's warm. And like I said, it's freaking Chanel. I don't know why people have such an issue with what I'm wearing tonight.

"Because red is going to look so much better on you, and it'll help us win." He smirks.

"Wearing red is going to help you win? How, exactly?" I lift a questioning brow even as my arm reaches out to accept the jersey.

"It's good luck," Travis says.

I glance at Harper and she just stares right back at me with wide eyes. I can see it on her face, though. Exactly what she's thinking.

Don't argue. Just put on the damn jersey.

Travis takes hold of my hand. "Follow me," he says without actually giving me a choice.

It's not until we turn a corner that I realize my friend isn't behind us. She's let this hulk of a man drag me off to God only knows where, to do God only knows what. Alone.

"You can change here," Travis tells me, nodding at a small cubicle space. "No one will see you."

kylie Kent

I stare at him. I don't know why I'm playing along. But I am. I undo the button of my coat. "I'm wearing clothes under this, just so you know. It's not like anyone would see anything anyway," I say while shrugging out of the sleeves and handing him my coat.

Travis doesn't hide the way his gaze runs up and down my body. "Yeah, that's not an outfit I want all my teammates seeing you in."

I roll my eyes. "There's nothing wrong with what I'm wearing," I tell him as I tug the jersey over my head and flatten it in place. Then I hold out my hand to take my coat back.

Travis keeps it in his firm grip. "I'll return it after the game. Better yet, I'll buy you a red one."

"I'm going to freeze my ass off out there in this," I whine.

"I know a way you can stay warm." He smirks.

"How?"

He leans in to whisper in my ear. "Just think of all the ways I'm going to fuck you after this game."

"You seem really sure of yourself," I tell him.

"I am. Now, come on. It's time to get back out there." He takes my hand and leads me around the corner, stopping before he turns to me. "I didn't catch your name."

"I'll tell you my name after you win tonight. If you lose, then... well... guess you'll be left wondering."

"I don't plan on losing."

"Nobody ever plans on losing." I shrug before pivoting on my heel and heading out of the locker room with Harper in tow.

She leads us back to our seats in front of the ice. "I can't believe you just got O'Neil's jersey," she shouts at me.

"Why?"

"You have no idea what just happened in there," she says.

"I met a superstitious hockey player who had a fit because I wasn't wearing red," I tell her.

"Oh, girl, no. You were just claimed by Travis freaking O'Neil."

"I didn't get claimed by anyone. Besides, he doesn't even know who I am. When he finds out, he'll want this jersey back and then he'll want to forget he ever met me." It's the way it always is. Guys find out my last name and they run. Or they hang around long enough to accidentally "run into" one of my family members. And then I never hear from them again.

"Yeah, I think Travis is gonna be different. I've got a feeling." Harper sighs.

Everyone stands when the players start coming out onto the ice again. And Number Nine looks right at me and waves. Travis waves. At me. At least I think he's waving at me.

Chapter Two

As soon as she walked out of the locker room, the guys started in on me. I don't care, though. They can say whatever the fuck they wanna say about it. I'm probably out of my mind. I just claimed a chick whose name I don't even know.

She doesn't realize that I've put my mark on her. I saw her sitting there next to the team's newest PT hire and couldn't stop staring. It's not just the girl's looks that held me captive. There's something about her. Something I can't put my finger on. Sure, it doesn't hurt that she's hot as fuck. Long light-brown hair, tanned skin, dark-brown eyes. Her lips painted a deep shade of red. I couldn't help but want to see if that lipstick would smear.

I've never wanted to kiss a woman so much. It's like I was aching for it.

"You do know who she is, don't ya?" Harrison, the team's goalie, asks me as we're walking down the tunnel.

"Nope, I don't even know her name. What I do know is that she's going to be mine," I tell him.

"Yeah, good luck with that. I'll be sure to bring the flowers to your funeral," he says right before his skates hit the ice.

I shake off his words. I don't know what he's going on about. I also don't care. My eyes go straight to where she's sitting. I raise a gloved hand and wave at her. Her palm lifts ever so slightly, like she's unsure what she should be doing. After skating around, I head back to the bench. I'm not on the starting line. Her head turns in my direction. When the anthem begins to play, she focuses her attention on the flag. I can see her lips moving to the words of the song.

I force myself to stop all thoughts of her and get my head in the game. I can't be distracted. We need to win. I have a name to get and hopefully a number too. I don't plan on going home without a win *and* that woman tonight.

When my line's called up, I jump over the bench, my legs pumping as I chase the opposing player currently in possession of the puck. I quickly check him against the boards and pass to Melvin, who takes off down the ice. I'm right behind him. He shoots, and I watch as the puck rebounds off the top of the net. It flies back towards me. I catch it with my glove, drop it, and pass to my left. Logan shoots and lands that little black disk into the back of the net.

The lights go red, horns blare through the arena, and the crowd goes fucking wild. I jump on Logan and celebrate the score with a tap on his helmet. When I pivot back around, I look out to the crowd. Right to her. The girl in my jersey. She's on her feet, clapping her hands and cheering along with the rest of them.

Third period has us up by one. I'm on the edge of my seat, watching my boys out there fighting for that puck. Defending our lead. There're two minutes left on the clock. A new line goes out and they manage to regain control of the ice. One minute. I look over to where she's sitting. But she's not there.

Where'd she go?

Harper's gone too. Fuck, how did I miss it when she left?

The buzzer goes off, drawing my attention to my teammates. We won. I follow the guys over the bench as we celebrate our latest victory, while I continue to scan the crowd for her. Then I remember that I have her coat. She's going to want that back.

Sure enough, when I make it to the locker room, my girl's waiting for me with Harper. Her eyes connect with mine and I smile. I walk right over to her and drop my helmet to the floor. My hand reaches behind her neck and I arch her face upwards before slamming my lips onto hers. My tongue delves into her mouth, tasting every inch of her.

When I pull back again, she smiles up at me. "Congrats. You won," she says.

"Don't you worry. By the end of the night, you'll be the one winning, babe." I wink at her.

"I just came to get my coat." She shrugs.

"We won, which means I get your name now."

"Liliana Valentino," she says with an expectant look on her face. Like I'm supposed to recognize that name or something. I don't.

"It's nice to meet you, Lili. I'm Travis." I hold out a palm.

She places her small hand in mine. "Uh-huh. Can I have my coat back now?"

"You can. I'm just gonna jump in the shower real quick. Wait for me," I tell her, and without pausing for an answer, I walk past her towards the stalls. I don't think I've ever gotten out of my gear so fast before. I don't want to risk her leaving without me.

Liliana. It's a pretty name. I make quick work of showering before wrapping a towel around my waist and heading back out. Lili is in the corner with Harper and the rest of the team's sports med department. She has her back to me. But when she senses my approach, she turns around and her eyes widen.

I smirk. It's not the first time I've seen that look on a woman's face. Although seeing it on hers is

21

somehow a lot more satisfying, especially when she's wearing my jersey. Lili turns her head back around. She can pretend that I don't affect her. It's too late, though. I already know I do.

I throw on a pair of sweats and a team hoodie. And I'm sliding my feet into my shoes when Logan nudges me in the side. "You in some kinda hurry?" he asks me.

"I am actually."

"You know, because I'm your friend and you're a damn good player, I'm going to give you some sound advice, advice you should take," he says, grabbing my attention. "Don't go there. No chick is worth risking your life. And trust me when I say touching that one is more dangerous than stepping out in front of a bus."

"Why?" I ask him.

"That's Liliana Valentino," he says.

"I know her name, idiot. Why is she so dangerous?"

"Valentino, as in *the* Valentinos." He puts her last name in air quotes.

"Still not getting it." I shrug one shoulder, already bored with everyone's dramatics.

"Okay, well, I warned you. So when it blows up

in your face, I can honestly say I told you so," he grunts before walking away.

"Congrats, boys. Morning skate, 0700 hours. Don't be late," Coach yells out above the chatter of the locker room. Everyone is on cloud nine. There's nothing like winning.

Picking up Lili's coat from my locker, I walk over to her. "You ready to get out of here?"

She jumps at the sound of my voice. When she spins back in my direction, her lips tip up at one side. "You sure you want to take me home?"

I run my eyes up and down her body. "Never been more sure of anything in my life, babe," I tell her.

"Okay then, but we're going to your place. Mine is... well, it'd be like walking through a minefield." She laughs.

Taking hold of her hand, I lead her out of the locker room and towards the bank of elevators that will bring us to the undercover garage. "Did you drive here?" I ask her.

"Nope. I came with Harper," she says.

I nod my head, unlock my Jeep, and open the passenger door. "Your chariot awaits, princess." I grin while tipping an imaginary hat.

"Not a princess. But thank you," she mumbles as she slides onto the seat.

Chapter Three

I should warn him. Tell him who I am. It's obvious he has no idea, but I kind of like that. I like not being known as the mafia princess. As the *Valentino Princess*. It's refreshing.

Or maybe he does know and just doesn't care.

If that were true, he'd be the first person I've come across who, one, didn't fear my family. And two, didn't want to try to gain something through me. I've gotten used to it. I've never really known any differently.

Right now, the only vibes I'm getting from Travis are the ones telling me just how much he wants to get in my pants. Which I'm totally on board with. A girl has needs, and those needs went into overdrive the moment I saw him in nothing but a white towel. Water dripping down his body. And what a freaking body it is.

My legs squeeze together, trying to ease some of the building pressure.

"You doing okay over there?" Travis asks, humor in his voice.

"Just fine. How far is your place?"

"About twenty. Why?"

"No reason," I tell him. I can wait twenty minutes before I jump his bones. It's only twenty minutes. I can do this. I try to distract myself, think about anything other than the hunk sitting next to me.

Travis's hand lands on my upper thigh. I jump at the contact. "Are you sure you're okay? You don't have to come home with me, you know. I can drive you to your place," he offers.

"I'm fine. I just... I'm horny, okay? So if you could speed this whole thing up a bit, I'd appreciate it," I admit.

His neck snaps in my direction and there's a huge smile on his face.

"Don't look like you won the golden ticket. I like sex. It could be with anyone really. You just happen to be the one I'm going home with tonight." It's a lie. Not the whole liking sex part; the I'd go home with anyone part. I don't. I wouldn't. But I needed to wipe that cocky-ass smirk off his face somehow. And it worked.

"So you do this often then?" he says, his tone much more serious.

"Not really." I shrug.

The rest of the ride is silent, the feel of his thumb rubbing up and down my jean-clad thigh driving me insane. I think he knows exactly what his touch is doing to me too.

Travis parks the car. I don't have the chance to grab the handle when he's jumping out and prying my door open from the other side. And before I manage to take a step forward, my back is pressed up against metal and his mouth finds my neck. My fingers grip his hoodie, holding onto him.

"Just so we're clear. I'm going to fucking ruin you for life. No other man will ever be able to give you the kind of pleasure I plan to give you tonight." His raspy voice sends shivers right down my spine.

"You talk a big game. Sure you can deliver on that?"

"Let's find out." He steps away and I'm suddenly left cold, wanting to pull him back against me. I drop my hands from his hoodie.

Travis wraps his arm around my shoulders and starts leading me towards the elevators. That's when I notice where we are and dig my feet into the ground.

"You live here?" I ask him.

"Yeah, last I checked."

"What floor? What apartment?"

"Fifteen, apartment twenty-two."

"I'm going to follow you up. Give me five minutes," I tell him.

"Why?"

"Just... trust me. If I go in there with you, the night is not going to end the way you're expecting." Shit. How do I tell him my family owns this building? That they have cameras everywhere and the men who monitor them aren't just regular security guards. They work for my father. They're his soldiers.

If they notice me going inside with a guy, they're going to report that back. But if I walk in by myself, no one will care. They'll just think I'm using the penthouse.

"Okay. See you in five." Travis pulls a card from his wallet. "Use this to get in," he says.

I nod my head while feeling like a complete idiot. But it's either this or risk having his door broken in. Travis looks back at me as he enters the elevator, and he keeps looking when the doors close on him. I briefly consider turning around and running. It's a very brief thought, before the need to ride that man until the sun comes up overtakes my better sense.

I wait a minute. Then I press the button on the elevator, praying that whoever is manning the cameras in this garage isn't watching or at the very least hasn't noticed that I'm here. I step into the elevator and press floor number fifteen. When I get to Travis's apartment, I swipe the card he gave me and push the door open. The next thing I know, I'm being swooped up into a pair of arms. Strong, muscular arms.

"Ah, what the hell?" I scream as I'm spun around and pushed up against the closest wall.

"I thought you'd changed your mind," Travis says, nuzzling my neck.

"I thought about it, for about half a second," I tell him as my arms wrap around his shoulders.

"What made you decide to come up?" he asks.

"The promise of being ruined for all mankind." I smile at him. "I need to see if your game is as good as your talk."

"Oh, babe, my game is way better than my talk." Travis picks me up. And my legs wrap around his waist as he walks us through his apartment. My body flies through the air and I land on something soft. Not something, his bed. Travis stares down at me. "I'm torn. I want to strip you naked, but I also want to fuck you while you're wearing my jersey," he says.

"Why not do both?" I challenge him. "Or are you a one-and-done kind of guy? It's okay if you are."

His eyebrows turn down at me. "No, I'm not. And both is exactly what I'm going to do." He reaches for my right leg and unzips my boot, tossing it onto the floor next to the bed before he repeats the process with my left side. Then he undoes my jeans and slides them, along with my panties, down my legs in one swoop.

"Fuck me," Travis hisses when his eyes land on my now-bare pussy.

"I was kind of hoping that's what you'd be doing to me." I laugh.

Travis's hands grip my thighs, pushing my legs open wider. "Fuck yes, I'm going to fuck you so good you'll be lucky to walk tomorrow," he says, talking at my vagina and not my face.

I can feel myself get wetter with his dirty promises. "Best get to work then," I tell him.

Travis removes his hands from my legs. He pulls his hoodie off and then slides his sweats down. Leaving absolutely nothing to my imagination.

Holy freaking cow!

I've heard of the term *hung like a horse*. But, sweet baby Jesus, what the fuck is that thing dangling between his legs? Well, not so much dangling anymore.

Maybe I'm not as sexually experienced as I thought I was, because I've never come face-to-face with anything like Travis's cock before now. Seriously, is this guy from outer space?

"Like what you see?" Travis smirks as he looks down at me. His fist wraps around his cock, pumping it up and down slowly. The tip glistens with precum. My tongue darts out and I lick my lips.

"I want to taste," I blurt out the thought I was intending to keep to myself.

Travis's smile widens. "All in good time, babe." He winks at me again. Then I watch as he walks around the bed and opens a drawer in the nightstand before pulling out a string of foil packets.

Chapter Four

My teeth tear through the foil packet, the first of many, as I look down on this insanely beautiful creature currently sprawled out on my bed. And I realize I'm harder than I've ever been in my life. Fuck, I want to get inside her.

Rolling the condom over my cock, I kneel on the bed between her thighs. Then I drag my fingers up the center of her slit. "Fuck, you're wet," I hiss out, feeling the evidence of her need.

"Sorry," she says while a shy blush creeps up her cheeks.

"Nothing to be sorry about, babe. It's a good thing. It's fucking fantastic." I bring my fingers up to my mouth and suck them clean. "Fucking delicious."

I should take my time, and I will. Just not right now. Right now, I need to get inside her. I lift the hem of my jersey. I've never fucked a chick wearing my jersey before. This is a first for me, and I'm left wondering why. It's fucking hot as hell.

Gripping my cock, I line it up with her entrance. Lili's eyes widen. "You ready for this?" I ask her. "Because if you want to back out, now's the time. Once I'm in, I don't think I'm going to want to stop." I pause to look at her. "I would, though. You know, if you told me you wanted to stop, I'd stop." I need her to know that she's the one in control here.

"I want this." Lili's teeth dig into her bottom lip. "What if it doesn't fit? I know that sounds stupid, but that thing is bigger than my largest vibe and that's a tight fit." Her cheeks turn a shade darker when she says this.

"I'll go slow, but it's gonna fit, babe. Promise."

I lean forward. My lips press onto her mouth, and my tongue pushes inside, swirling in rhythm with hers. I'm not sure I've ever enjoyed kissing a chick as much as I'm enjoying this. My cock is rock-fucking-hard and begging for me to slam into her. Like it knows where it wants to be, the tip of my cock lines up with her entrance and I slowly start to slide inside her. My lips leave hers, and I look down at where our bodies are connected.

"Fuck, you're a tight little thing," I hiss through my teeth. Then I pull out and slide back in a little farther.

"It's not me. It's you. That thing is not a normal size, Travis," Lili says. She spreads her legs even wider before her ankles hook behind my back.

I smile. "Thanks." I wink at her as I pull out and push back in again.

She's tight, but her worries are unwarranted. Her pussy fits my cock like a fucking glove. I can feel every bit of her hugging me. Squeezing me. And it's fucking amazing. The next thrust has me bottoming out. I'm all in. So I still and allow her body time to adjust.

"You okay?" I ask while peering down at what has to be one of the most perfect faces I've ever seen.

"Uh-huh, you can move. I'm good. Better than good," she says, her pussy spasming around me.

My eyes close. *Think about cats. Think about Grams. Think about anything but how fucking good she feels.* I will not be a one-pump chump.

Pulling out, I thrust back in. Harder. Lili moans and I'd do anything to hear that sound coming from her lips again. My hand trails down her left leg, unwrapping it from behind my back and lifting it until her knee is pressing against her chest. Her body opens up for me in this position, and her moans get louder. My hips twist as I thrust and grind against her. My speed increases, and her mass of light-brown hair sprawls out across my navy sheets. Her eyes, so fucking green they sparkle like emeralds, are wide. Staring back at me.

"I'm going to..." she says.

"Let it happen. Come for me," I tell her before doubling my efforts.

Her pussy spasms around my cock. And, fuck, I can't hold back much longer. When she screams through her orgasm, I hear the horns. See the smoke. Fucking goal! Her face flashes a light red.

Fuck me, I come right after her. Freezing while buried deep inside her. I'm reluctant to leave this newfound slice of heaven. My lips find hers. Both of us breathless. Each of us dueling for ownership as our tongues tangle together.

"This is just the start," I tell Lili as I pull out. "I'm going to take care of this." I remove the condom from my cock. "When I get back in here, I want to see you completely naked and waiting for me." I rush into the bathroom and throw the condom in the trash can. I quickly wash my hands, too eager to get back to her.

When I walk back into the room, she's pulling her shirt over her head.

"Need a hand?" I ask because, honestly, stripping this woman naked is like opening a Christmas gift. The excitement, the thrill of finding out what's underneath. I don't want to wait. I just want to tear into it. Into her.

"I got this," she says as she tosses her shirt on the ground, right on top of the jersey she was wearing.

I bend down to dig my phone out of my pocket. "Before we get started again, I'm going to need you to put your number in here." I unlock the screen and hand it over to her.

Lili's brows draw down. "Why?"

"Because I'm not risking waking up in the morning, you not being here and me not having a way to contact you."

"That happen often? Women leaving you in the middle of the night?" She smirks.

"It's never happened, but like I said, I'm not taking chances with you." I crawl onto the bed and sit in front of her. She's on her knees, wearing nothing but a black lace bra. I lean forward, barely a breath between us. "Start typing, Lili." I kiss my way across her collarbone as my hands reach behind her back and unclasp her bra.

She taps a few times before shoving my phone into my bare chest. "Here."

I straighten up, look at the screen, and press *call* on her name. The trill of a ringing cell phone comes from somewhere on the floor.

Lili raises her brows at me. "Didn't trust me?" She laughs.

"Just wanted to make sure you weren't tryin' to dodge me already, babe." I hang up. "Besides, now you have my number too." I drop my phone onto the bedside table.

"So can we get to the continued sexcapade part of the night now?"

"You want me to fuck you again, Lili?" I ask

while running a hand down her right arm. The straps of her bra fall to her wrists.

"Yes, I do," she says. Her chest pushes out slightly, in my direction. As if she's offering herself up to me. An offering I'm not going to turn down.

The sound of my alarm blaring through the darkened room has me slapping an arm out and trying to turn the damn thing off. I finally manage to hit the button. I know I have to get up. No amount of sleeping in is worth the hell I'd get from coach if I'm late to morning skate.

"Argh, what is that?" a voice next to me asks.

I look over. She's still here. "Sorry, alarm, babe. I have to go to work," I tell her.

"You play hockey. Pretty sure there aren't games scheduled at this ungodly hour," she grunts.

"Practice happens every morning." I roll over and kiss her forehead. "Make yourself at home. Feel free to stay and sleep. I'll be back around lunchtime if you want to wait."

"Mhmm," Lili mumbles as she snuggles deeper into the covers.

I force myself to get out of bed. It's never been fucking harder. I'd love to stay and go for round five with this woman. But the ice waits for no one. At least that's what Coach likes to tell us.

Chapter Five

As soon as consciousness seeps in, I remember where I am. I peek an eye open and find the space next to me empty. A vague memory of Travis saying he had to go somewhere is there in the back of my mind.

He left me in his apartment. Either he's

extremely trusting or the guy's an idiot. Probably both, considering he has no idea who I am and he left me here. Alone. The itch to get up and snoop is almost too much. I peer up at the ceiling. There are no obvious cameras that I can see. Although, remembering what I let this man do to my body last night, I probably should have been looking for those *before* I got naked.

Speaking of, I should also get up and get out of his place before he comes back. Save myself and him that awkward "morning after" conversation that I'm sure neither of us wants to have.

I throw the blankets aside, and the second my feet hit the floor, I feel it. The way he used my body. I'm sore, but in a good way. Like I've been thoroughly fucked. Because, let's be honest, that's exactly what Travis did to me last night. He came through on every single dirty promise he whispered into my ear.

I find my discarded clothes folded and placed on the single chair in the corner of his room. I really want a shower. I took one last night with Travis, but we did a lot more than just wash off in there. I put on my bra and then my shirt. Then I reach for my jeans and tug them up my thighs. My underwear is missing, not that I would have put them on again anyway.

I bend down and search under the bed. They're not there. I do find his jersey on the floor though. The same one I wore last night. So I pick it up and slide it over my head. When I look over, I see that my boots and socks are tucked neatly against the wall.

When did he have time to arrange all my stuff? I didn't hear a single thing after he said he was going to work.

I grab my boots, figuring I can at the very least sneak up to the family penthouse and shower before going home. Make it to the open living room and freeze. There's a woman in Travis's kitchen.

Shit. Please tell me I didn't fuck a married man. I'm not the *other woman* kind of girl.

She looks up. "Oh my." Her hand comes to her chest. She's an older woman, around my mom's age. "I'm so sorry, darling. I didn't know anyone was here."

"Ah..." I open my mouth but I have no idea what to say. I don't know who this person is.

"I'm Frances, Travis's mother. I didn't wake you, did I? He didn't mention anyone was here," she says, already walking around the counter and heading in my direction.

"Ah, I'm Liliana. And I was just leaving. I'm sorry." I also have no idea what I'm apologizing for.

Maybe for screwing her son's brains out and having her find me looking like a tramp about to make the walk of shame out of his apartment?

"Liliana, such a beautiful name," she hums. "Come sit down. I was just about to make tea. You want one? Or how about some coffee?" She waves to the counter. "I drop off groceries for Travis. Because, well, I'm afraid if I don't, he'll just eat crap." She shrugs. "You are insanely beautiful. But you already know that. How do you take your tea?" The woman hasn't stopped talking or moving about the kitchen.

"I really do need to go. I'm sorry, Mrs. O'Neil," I repeat.

"It's just Frances, darling. And no need to apologize. I'm sure this is not how anyone expects to meet their boyfriend's mother," she says.

"Oh, Travis and I ... we aren't." I shake my head. How do I explain I just fucked her son and have no intentions of seeing him again?

"I'm not that old, darling. I know how you kids work these days. No labels and all that nonsense. But trust me... if my son left you asleep in his bed, in his apartment, then he likes you a whole lot. Which means this little meeting between us would have happened eventually."

I still don't know what to do here. What to say. I

don't want to be rude, but I really do need to go home. "I'm sure it would have." I smile at her. Travis's mom seems nice. A lot nicer than what my father would be to her son if the roles were reversed.

My own mother is a total sweetheart. She'd be all over Travis, trying to make sure he's comfortable and is properly fed. My father? Not so much. He'd likely call my uncles over to help him string the poor guy up by his ankles in the basement.

"Well, now that we've met, let's not be strangers," Frances says. "I'm sorry if I woke you, darling."

"You didn't. It was really great meeting you. But I have to dash out," I tell her.

"Oh, that's quite all right. Have a great day, Liliana." Frances smiles at me, and I wave awkwardly at her as I walk to the door.

I don't release the breath I was holding until I'm in the elevator descending to the garage, deciding it's probably best to just get out of this building before I run into any more of Travis's family. Or worse yet, the man himself.

I find one of my dad's cars and jump in. The keys are always inside. No one is stupid enough to steal a car with one of our Valentino plates.

I get the side-eye from two soldiers as I sneak into the house. I'm not stupid. I know there's no real *sneaking* involved. Within minutes, my father will know I'm only just getting home. But if I can manage to make it to my room without him seeing me, I know I'll have at least a few hours of peace before he comes knocking at my door. More than likely after my mother has calmed him down a bit.

"Stop right there! Where the fuck are you crawling in from?" The voice, although rough and deep, doesn't belong to my father. I glance over one shoulder and my glare lands on my brother. My *little* brother, mind you, who has taken on the role of the older sibling for some unknown reason.

"I was out," I tell him and roll my eyes.

"Obviously," Alessandro says. "Where were you?"

"Nowhere you need to know about." I smirk at him.

"Wait... What the hell are you wearing?" He's staring at me with wide eyes. "Is that...? Holy shit, that's an O'Neil jersey," he gasps, and I watch my brother's jaw drop.

Alessandro is a major hockey fan. Most of my family is, while I've never seen the appeal. Until now. "Huh, what do you know? It is."

"Where'd you get it?"

"I went to the game with Harper last night." I fold my arms over my chest.

"You didn't get that jersey from no pro shop, Lil. Who gave it to you?" Alessandro steps closer. His hand reaches out and he spins me around. "Holy fucking shit," he hisses as soon as his gaze lands on my back.

"What?" I peek over one shoulder, trying to see what he sees.

"It's signed. Travis fucking O'Neil signed this jersey."

"Okay..." I draw out as I step aside and spin around. "What is wrong with you?"

"You're wearing a signed O'Neil jersey, Lil. Do you have any idea how rare that is? I'll give you a hundred cold for it." Alessandro nods, already reaching for his phone and pulling up his banking app.

"What? No! You're out of your mind. It's just a

hockey jersey. It's not a big deal." I shake my head at him.

"Two hundred."

Two hundred thousand dollars for a signed jersey? He has to be shitting me.

"No. But next time I see Travis, I'll be sure to ask him to sign a piece of scrap paper for you." I laugh and then immediately clamp my mouth shut, realizing my mistake.

"Next time you see Travis? How the fuck do you know Travis O'Neil?" Alessandro narrows his glare at me.

"Yeah, you really don't want to know the answer to that question, little brother." I grin.

Alessandro groans. Like he's in physical pain. "Do not make me have to kill my favorite hockey player, Lil. Damn it."

I don't respond, simply quirking a brow instead.

"No. No. No! You are not..." He shakes his head.

"I'd love to stay and chat, but I got shit to do. Shit that doesn't include standing around here watching you try to come to terms with the fact that I may or may not have screwed your favorite hockey player." I pivot on my heel and continue down the hall, as my little brother tosses profanities at my back.

Chapter Six

Practice was grueling. All I wanted to do was crawl back into bed with the hot-as-sin woman I left behind in my apartment. It didn't help that I was running on two hours of sleep. And let's just say... I could have skipped this morning's practice with the amount of cardio I put in last night.

"I'm not walking out with you, man," Logan says, stopping short as we're about to exit the rink.

"What's wrong with you?" I flick him a glance as I push the door open.

"I'm not risking becoming target practice for any stray bullets that happen to be aimed your way."

"Are you on something?" My brows draw down. I don't know what the fuck's wrong with him.

"Nope, but you must be. Seeing as you thought it was a good idea to take the Valentino Princess home last night. That's the single most dangerous thing you could do in this city, man."

I blink at him.

"Come on, you've been here for three years. You can't seriously tell me you haven't heard of the Valentinos?"

"I've heard of them, sure. But I still have no idea what you're going on about or what it has to do with bullets."

"They're in the mob, you idiot. That girl's father is the underboss of the Valentino Crime Family, fuckwit," he huffs. "And you took her home and did God only knows what. Which means you're as good as dead when her father or any one of her uncles finds out."

"You're being dramatic." I shake my head. "I'll catch you tomorrow."

"Or I'll catch you at your funeral," he hollers back as the door closes behind me.

A few minutes later, I'm sliding into my car and pulling out my phone. I open Google and type in the words *Valentino* and *New York*. A shit-ton of articles come up about Lili's family. I shouldn't be reading them, but Logan has me curious.

Are they really part of the mob? And if they are, do I care?

The answer to that last one is a solid *fuck no*.

Tossing my cell onto the passenger seat, I start up the engine as the events of last night replay in my head, like a fucking porno on the big screen.

Fuck, I want her again.

The moment I pull up to my building, I jump out of my car and head straight to my apartment, making a beeline for my bedroom. Only to find the bed empty. I look to the chair where I left her clothes, sans her underwear because I kept those babies, and realize she's gone.

She fucking left.

I drop my bag on the floor and walk back out to

the kitchen. There's a note on the counter from my mom telling me to call her. I open the fridge and smile. She stocked my fridge. I let her think I'm hopeless when it comes to taking care of myself because nothing compares to my ma's homemade cooking.

I dig my phone out of my pocket and do my best to ignore the fact that my dick is half-hard. I was expecting to come home and slide right back into Lili, not find my bed empty and my fridge full. I dial my mom's number. She picks up on the third ring.

"Travis, I dropped some groceries off," she says in way of greeting.

"I saw. Thanks, Ma."

"I also met your friend," she singsongs.

"What friend?"

"Liliana, pretty little thing. I like her."

Oh my god, no wonder she fucking ran.

"What'd you say to her?" I ask my mother with a groan.

"Nothing! Just introduced myself. You should bring her home for dinner this weekend."

"Ma, I just met her last night. I don't think we're at the *dinner at the parents' house* phase of things yet."

"But I've already met her, and I like her. So bring

her to dinner," Mom says in her *don't argue with me* tone.

"Maybe one day. Thanks for the meals and groceries, Ma. I gotta go," I tell her. "I love you."

"Love you, Travis. Talk later," she says.

I run a hand down my face. How the fuck do I salvage things with Lili now? She met my mom. I left her alone in my apartment and my mother turns up. God, could this shit get any more embarrassing?

Without overthinking it too much, I find Lili's number in my phone. I stored it in my contacts as *Sweet Lili*, because she tastes so fucking sweet. Her whole personality—at least what I know of it so far—is sweet. Seeing her cheer me on when I was out on that ice did something to me. I want her at every fucking game. I want to see her face light up with excitement. I want her as my number one cheerleader.

Hitting the dial button, I wait. And wait. I'm about to abort mission when the line finally connects. "Hello?" Her voice is quiet, husky, like she's just waking up.

"Did I wake you, babe?"

"Who is this?" she asks.

"How many fucking guys call you *babe*?" I fire

back. "Actually... forget that. I don't care because they're irrelevant now that you've got me."

"Travis?"

"The one and only, babe. Were you sleeping? It's the middle of the day."

"Someone kept me up all night," she grumbles. "I'm tired."

"I don't recall you telling me to stop." I smile into the phone, while grabbing a bottle of water out of the fridge, and head into my living room. "What are you doing tonight? I want you again."

"You want me again? Not *I want to see you again*?" She laughs, sounding much more alert.

"Both."

"I can't tonight. I have plans."

"Cancel them," I tell her.

Lili laughs louder, and I can hear the ruffling of sheets. "My brother caught me coming home this morning. He offered me two hundred grand for your signed jersey," she says, then adds, "Also, I kept your jersey."

"It's yours to keep. Take his money. I'll get you another one."

"Nope, I'm not giving it to him. He's a big fan, by the way."

"Does that mean he's not gonna kill me?" I ask her.

"I wouldn't go that far. He looked really torn between having to play the protective brother role and fan-girling over his favorite player."

"I'm your brother's favorite player?" I quirk a brow even though I know she can't see me.

"You were, before he found out you fucked me."

"So, how about tonight?"

"Give me one good reason I should cancel my plans and meet up with you instead?"

"Easy. Orgasms. As in *multiple*," I tell her, my dick hardening at the thought.

"Mmm, tempting. You were pretty good at giving me those. But I really can't. I have to meet my cousin for dinner and I can't blow her off for orgasms, no matter how much I might want to."

"Come over when you're done," I try again.

"What about tomorrow?"

"I can't. We have an away game. I gotta be on a flight first thing."

"Where are you going?" she asks me.

"Nashville."

"Okay, I'll text you when I'm done with my cousin and see if you're still awake," Lili says.

My fist pumps up like I just scored the winning

goal. And, in a lot of ways, I fucking did. "I'll be awake, babe. See you soon." I hang up and toss my cell onto the coffee table.

Picking up the TV remote, I start flicking through channels. Trying to find something to watch. Something to occupy my time so I'm not just sitting here thinking about a woman I'm not going to see until later tonight.

My phone vibrates. I snatch it back up and see a message from her.

SWEET LILI:

I met your mom this morning. She seems nice.

ME:

She is nice. Sorry about that, by the way. I forgot she was coming over.

SWEET LILI:

It will go down as the most awkward walk of shame I've ever experienced.

ME:

There's no shame in what we did, Lili.

SWEET LILI:

Uh-huh, so you want to meet my folks after a night of screwing my brains out?

ME:

Wouldn't bother me. Parents tend to love me anyway.

SWEET LILI:

My father doesn't love anyone who isn't family. LOL.

ME:

I'd win him over, eventually...

How did we go from talking about hooking up tonight to discussing meeting the family? And why the fuck am I not running scared at the thought of this whole thing developing into something more serious?

Chapter Seven

She's late, but I'm not surprised. My younger cousin is never on time. Aurora lives by her own set of rules. I should find out what my Zia Savvy ate when she was pregnant with that girl and avoid whatever it is whenever I decide to have kids of my own. Because the world doesn't need more offspring like my cousin. At just eighteen, she's seen more trouble than all of us put together. And there are a lot of us.

I scroll through my phone, mindlessly looking at my social feeds to pass the time. Aurora will be here soon. She may be late, but she always shows.

"Shit, have you been waiting long? I'm sorry," she says, as if on cue.

"Not long. What held you up?"

"You don't want to know." Aurora gives me that devilish smirk she's mastered.

"Tell me the oldies aren't about to bust in any moment because you've done something reckless again?" I plead with her. It wouldn't be the first time.

"They're not. Don't be so dramatic, Lil. I covered my tracks." She shrugs, and I huff out a sigh.

"I have plans after dinner and I really don't have time to be saving you from your parents," I tell her.

"Pfft, as if I need anyone to save me." She laughs before quickly changing the subject. "So plans, huh? What are they? And can you order me a cosmo?" She bats her eyelashes at me.

"Nothing, and no." I pick up my glass of wine and sip at it just to annoy her. She's eighteen, but no stranger to alcohol. Even so, I refuse to buy it for her, and anyone who knows what's good for them won't either. Which only makes it more of a wonder as to how she always seems to have a stash of liquor somewhere in her bedroom.

"Fine," she grunts.

"I'm assuming there's a reason for this impromptu dinner?" I ask, trying to get right to the point.

"Can't I just want to have dinner with my cousin for the sake of having dinner?"

"You can, but it's you, and you don't do anything without an agenda."

"I think Nonno is getting ready to hand over the reins to Zio Theo," she says bluntly.

My glass pauses midair. This is huge. "What makes you think that?"

"I overheard Nonno and Nonna talking about it." Aurora lifts a single shoulder.

"You mean you eavesdropped on what I'm assuming was a private conversation?"

"Same thing."

"Nonno isn't even that old yet," I say. "You don't think he's sick, do you?"

Aurora shakes her head. "No, I don't think so."

"Why would he be handing things over so early, then?"

"No idea, but it's what I heard."

If what she says is true, my world is about to be turned upside down when my father becomes the Don. He's the current underboss, so it's only one step up. But it's still a huge change. I wonder if he's ready for it. Especially so soon.

"Well, whatever happens, it'll be fine," I tell Aurora.

"What if my dad ends up having to be the new underboss?" she asks.

My Zio Matteo is a criminal defense attorney, so is my Zia Livvy. They have a firm together. My uncle may be a made man but he's also chosen to keep his hands clean—as much as he can anyway.

"They're not going to do that. It doesn't make sense. Besides, there are other options."

"Well, it's not going to be Zio Romeo," Aurora muses. He's the current mayor and more on the up-and-up than most politicians.

"Zio Luca is my bet," I suggest with a nod.

"Makes sense. Now, enough family chitchat. Who and what is the thing you're doing after dinner?"

"Again, nothing you need to know about."

"Come on, you know I'm going to follow you and find out anyway if you don't tell me." Aurora says.

"Do not follow me." I direct a manicured finger

at her. "I met someone last night. I'm seeing him again tonight."

"Does he have a name?"

"He does, but that's all you're getting out of me. I don't want him scared off just yet."

"Lorenzo says someone who can be scared off isn't worth a dime of your time in the first place," she counters, referring to her eldest brother.

"He's right," I agree.

My head is spinning as I consider what my cousin told me at dinner. My father taking my grandfather's place isn't news. But the timing is. I don't know how it will shift the dynamics in my family, or if it will at all. What I do know is that I'm going to make the most of the time I have with Travis before he finds out he's sleeping with a mafia princess and runs for the hills. Because, let's face it, my father is scarier than the devil himself.

I don't blame anyone for running. It's the best form of self-preservation.

I lift my hand over the door, knock, and take a

step back. I told Travis I was going to text him, but I decided to just rock up instead. I hear his footsteps on the other side of the door and then it swings open.

Travis smiles before his mouth drops into a frown. "How'd you get up here?" he asks while scanning the empty hallway.

"I, ah, my family owns the building. We have a penthouse here," I tell him and wait to see if he's still going to invite me in.

His arm snakes out and wraps around my waist. "Get the fuck in here. I've been waiting for you," he says. The door slams shut right as Travis's lips descend onto mine.

He ravages my mouth, pushing his tongue past the seam. There isn't anything soft or slow about his kiss. It's rough, hard, and fast. Like he's starving and I'm the thing he's been craving. My arms close around his neck, pulling him tighter against my body. And I moan when I feel his hard-on press into my stomach. I can still feel the effects of last night's encounter. But that doesn't stop me from wanting him again. My feet are lifted off the ground, and we're moving through his apartment. Travis doesn't break the kiss as his tongue duels with mine and his hands palm the flesh of my ass.

"Fuck, it's been a long-ass day without you," he says into my mouth.

I don't really know what to think of that. So I pull on the ends of his hair instead, deepening the kiss. My body is lifted higher and then I'm falling. Travis follows me down, and we collapse onto his mattress.

This is not how this is going to go this time around. I want him. I want to get the most of this body of his before it's too late. My legs hook around his waist and I turn, flipping him onto his back. His eyes widen as I straddle him. I lift the hem of my sweater over my head and toss the material behind me.

"You hungry, babe?" Travis asks with a smirk.

"Starved," I tell him and claw at his shirt. He props himself up on his elbows and helps me peel the fabric from his body.

"Well, now that you have me in front of you, what are you going to taste first?" he lifts a questioning brow.

I drag my nails down the middle of his torso. Damn, this man is cut to perfection.

"I'm going to start here," I say, circling my fingers around his nipple. "And then work my way down to... here." I trace that same finger around his belly button. His stomach muscles flex and his eyes darken as I slip my hand under the waistband of his sweats and fist his cock. "Then I'm going to taste this." I pump twice before releasing my grip and pulling my hand back.

Travis groans as he squeezes my hips until he shifts his focus and unclasps my bra. "You have amazing tits." He palms them as soon as the straps slip down my shoulders.

"Thank you." My back arches into his touch. I almost forget my plans to run this show when he rolls my nipples through his fingertips. "Shit," I hiss.

I bend forward, forcing Travis to drop his hands, as my tongue darts out and I lick around his right nipple before sucking it into my mouth. His hips lift off the bed and his hard cock presses against my core. My skirt has already ridden up and my lace panties are doing nothing to hide my arousal. I don't stop, though.

Instead, I move across to the other nipple, flicking my tongue over the tip and then sucking hard. Travis combs his hands into my hair, fisting it as he holds the stray locks away from my face, and stares down at me. "I've never seen a more fucking beautiful sight."

I start making my way down his body, kissing,

licking, sucking, and biting. Until I position myself between his legs, reach back inside his sweats, and free his cock. Travis groans the moment my hand makes contact. The tip glistens with precum as I bend forward, stick my tongue out, and lick. He hardens in my grip. I continue along the underside and around the front again.

"Babe, stop fucking with me," he grinds out, and I smile up at him.

I like that I affect him just as much as he affects me. I open my mouth and take him as far back as I can manage while my hand wraps around the base to cover what's left over.

"Fuck me," Travis hisses and grinds against my face.

Hollowing out my cheeks, I suck up and down his length. Slowly. The feel of him in my mouth is arousing. I don't want to stop, but I need something for myself. So I reach down, between my own legs, and press my fingers to my clit as I continue to suck. I moan around his length.

"Fuck, nope, not happening," Travis grunts, forcing me to look up at him just as he tugs me up and his cock pulls free from my mouth.

"What's wrong?" I ask him.

"I'm not letting you get yourself off, babe. That's

my job," he says before spinning me around like a rag doll as he positions my body so that I'm on top of him, my ass inches from his face. "This will work better." He presses on my spine, guiding me forward again.

My hand returns to his cock, and I take him back into my mouth. Travis pushes my panties out of the way as he slides his fingers through my wet folds. I pause, losing myself to the pleasure.

"If you stop, I stop. Don't fucking stop," he warns.

I nod my head, because I have manners and all that. Never speak with your mouth full, am I right?

Travis's tongue circles around my clit, and I have to force myself to focus on the job at hand. I want to make him feel as good as he's making me feel. My thighs shake, my orgasm building fast, so I increase my efforts. Sucking harder and faster. I need him to come. I want him to lose control for me.

"Fuck, I'm coming." He taps my hip, but I don't stop.

I want him. I want all of him. And as soon as I feel the first squirt on my tongue, my own orgasm washes over me. I swallow as much as I can, while my body convulses with wave after wave of pleasure.

A few seconds later, we collectively fall back

onto the mattress, lying head to toe, each trying to catch our breath. Travis's hand lands on my thigh. "Fuck me, babe, that was so fucking hot," he says. "Five-minute intermission before the next act."

"Five minutes," I agree, because I still don't feel like I've had my fill of him.

Chapter Eight

My arms tighten around a body. A soft body. Smooth skin. And my nose buries into a neck. I breathe in a hint of vanilla and berry. "Lili," I whisper.

"This *waking up at the crack of dawn* thing needs to stop," she groans.

I open my eyes, reach out a hand, and brush the hair off her face. "The day is young. Why waste it?" I tell her before pressing my lips to her forehead. "Besides, I have to be at the team jet by noon and I want to take you to breakfast first."

Lili pops one eye open to glare at me. "You want to take me to breakfast? Like, in public?"

"Yeah. Why not?"

"People will see us," she states the obvious.

"So?"

"I'm not sure I want people to see us."

"Well, fuck, I'll try not to let that blow hit my ego, babe." I laugh. Although, deep down, I'm wondering what the fuck is so wrong with me she doesn't want anyone to see us together.

"It's not you. It's very much a *me* thing," she says, then adds, "Well, it's a *my family* thing. I don't want this to stop, and I know you're not going to want to see me again after you meet them. And that's okay. I get it. I come with a lot. But I want to be selfish and keep you a bit longer."

I'm speechless. Who in their right mind would leave this woman?

"Babe, I don't know what kind of fuckwits you've dated in the past, but it's going to take a lot more than meeting your family to send me packing." I shrug.

70

"We're not dating, Travis. I just meant the sex. I like the sex. You're kind of good at it."

"Just kind of? That's not what you were saying last night when you were screaming my name." My fingers trail across her collarbone, her smooth skin, up her throat before I tip her chin and force her to look at me. "Also, we *are* dating."

"And when did *we* decide that? We only just met."

"I decided. Just now. Come on and get that fine ass up so I can take you on our first official date." I slip out of bed before she can argue with me and give her ass a firm tap to get her moving.

"It's really not a good idea, Travis," she says.

"It'll be fine. Promise." I walk into my closet, fingering through a few hangers until I find what I'm looking for, and I pull it down. Then I walk out and I lay it over the bed. The same bed Lili hasn't moved from yet.

"A suit is a bit much for breakfast, don't you think?" she asks with an arched brow.

"I have a jet to catch and the suit is a requirement. After breakfast, I plan on driving you home and then heading straight to the hangar."

"Oh," she says. "Okay, I'm getting up. But I'm

warning you I'm not going to look nearly as good as you will in that." She gestures to the suit.

Forty minutes later, I'm navigating the garage with my hand locked on Lili's—she looks fucking sensational by the way. Her lips are painted with a fresh coat of red, her eyes are a darker gray color, and her hair is piled up in a high ponytail that I'm envisioning wrapping around my fist. She helped herself to one of my hoodies, pairing it with her black miniskirt from last night and some matching pumps.

My eyes travel up and down her body. "Fuck me, we should just go back inside," I groan.

Lili peers up at me. "Why?"

"Because I can't look at you and not think about fucking you," I tell her.

She smiles huge while her eyes take me in from head to toe. "Yeah, I get that."

"Liliana?" a deep voice calls out to her from across the garage.

I look over and see three men headed in our direction. I push Lili behind me, much to her annoyance it seems. She slaps my back and tries to step around me.

The three men stop in front of us, and before I can even consider moving, I have a gun pointed right at my head. "You have two seconds to get your fucking hands off my daughter, asshole," the guy in the middle grinds out between a tightly clenched jaw.

"Daddy, no!" Lili screams and rushes forward, planting herself between me and the barrel.

"Liliana, move out of the way," he says.

"Lili, move," I tell her at the same time.

"No. Stop. Oh my god! I'm calling Mom. This is insane." She ignores the gun still aimed at my skull and pivots towards the other two men flanking her father. "Do something, you idiots. Don't just stand there."

I don't take my eyes off the guy with the gun, though. Lili is way too fucking close to that loaded weapon and I don't fucking like it. "Babe, I really want you to move out of the way."

I watch as her father's jaw tick slightly. But other than that, his face is devoid of emotion. Maybe Logan was right. Maybe my ass really is about to get shot.

Doesn't matter. Still worth it. *She's* worth it. I

don't know her that well yet, but I always trust my gut. And my gut says this girl is worth all the trouble that comes with her last name.

Or I could just be out of my fucking mind.

"Pops, put the gun down. You're not shooting fucking Travis O'Neil," the youngest one in the bunch grunts while throwing a hand in my direction. I'm guessing he's Lili's brother.

"Come on, Theo, put it away." The third guy snatches the gun from her father's hand. "Too slow, bro." He laughs as he holds it just out of reach.

"I don't need that to kill him."

"Dad, stop. We're leaving," Lili growls while tugging at my arm.

"He's leaving. You're not," her father says.

"Actually, she is. If Lili wants to leave, no one is going to stop her from doing it," I tell him, regretting the words as soon as they're out of my mouth. And not because I don't mean them, but because it's disrespectful and my mother raised me better. "Sir," I add at the end. He is her father after all.

"And who do you think is going to stop me from keeping my daughter here? You?" he counters, looking me up and down.

"If I have to, for her, yes." I keep my gaze locked on his.

"Fucking hell. Lil, get him out of here before it's too late," the third guy steps between us with a forced sigh.

"Thanks, Zio Matteo. I *am* calling Mom, by the way. I hope you have a lot to do today. I wouldn't rush home," Lil says to her father, and it doesn't take a genius to hear the threat hanging in the air.

"Liliana, a word," he replies before dropping his glare on her and stepping aside.

Lili turns back to me. "I'll meet you at the car. Give me a second. Or, you know, if you want to leave without me, that's okay too." She doesn't look at me when she says that last part.

I reach out for her face and tip her head up again. "I'm not going anywhere without you, babe. I'll wait right here. Go talk to your dad."

"Do not touch him." Lili points at her uncle and then brother before storming past them, the click of her heels on the cement floor echoing behind her as she goes.

I watch on as she steps up to her father. He pulls her into a hug and her body sags against his chest.

"You know, if you weren't Travis fucking O'Neil, I would have let him shoot you."

Her brother's voice has me looking his way.

"Good to know," I tell him while holding out a hand. "I'm Travis."

He only leaves me hanging for a second before he returns the gesture. "Alessandro, her brother." He dips his head in Lili's direction, then adds, "Get a real good look at my face, because if you hurt her, it'll be the last thing you see and it won't matter what your name is."

"Right, well, I've seen far worse," I tell him. "I'm sure you've seen some of my teammates. Not all of them are as pretty as you are." Then I turn to the third guy and introduce myself. "Travis."

"Matteo, her uncle," he grunts and shakes my hand, though it's clear he doesn't want to.

"So... nice day, huh?" I ask, trying to kill the awkward silence that's settled between us.

"You're playing Nashville tomorrow, right?" Alessandro asks.

"We are."

"When do you play the Knights again?"

"Vancouver?" I question him.

"Who else?"

"Just checking. Two weeks," I tell him. I've been waiting for this game. My people have been in nego-tiations with the Vancouver Knights, looking to get me signed. I'm a free agent, and the Knights are it for me. I've been a fan since I was old enough to stay upright on a pair of skates.

"I'll give you one mil to knock Monroe on his ass at least three times when you play him," Alessandro says, and I laugh.

"Sorry, no can do. I don't take bribes." I shake my head. I'm not a dirty player. "But I'll knock him on his ass just because I can. That guy has a chip on his shoulder the size of fucking Texas." I smirk.

"Travis, let's go. My father is sorry for pointing a gun at you," Lili says when they approach a few minutes later. The look on Mr. Valentino's face tells me otherwise. The man is not the least bit sorry.

"Well, it was great meeting you all." I dip my head to Lili's brother and uncle before passing her father. "Sir." I nod and keep walking—or, more accurately, I let Lili drag me towards the car.

Chapter Nine

I keep looking over at Travis. He seems like he doesn't have a care in the world. He just came face-to-face with my father and didn't flinch. Like at all. And now he's taking me to breakfast, as if a gun wasn't just pointed at his head not even five minutes ago.

"You okay?" he asks. Picking up my hand and bringing it to his mouth, he kisses my knuckles.

"I'm pretty sure I should be asking you that question," I tell him.

"I asked you first, babe."

"Travis, my dad was *this close...*" I hold up my free hand, indicating the tiny space between my thumb and index finger. "This fucking close to blowing your head off, and you're asking if I'm okay?" I laugh. It's not funny. I'm not laughing because it's funny. It's more of a *I don't know what's fucking happening to my life* kind of laugh.

"Babe, answer the question. Are you okay?" he repeats.

"I don't know," I admit.

"Okay." Travis nods his head. "What can I do to help you be okay?"

"You're serious?" My neck snaps around to look at him so fast I'm surprised I don't pull a muscle.

"As a heart attack, babe. Tell me what I can do to help."

"I'm sorry. I should have said that first. I'm sorry my family is... a little intense."

Travis stops at a red light. He looks across at me with raised brows. "A little intense?"

"A lot intense," I clarify.

79

"It's fine. I'm bullet free and so are you. We're fine," he says.

"Just so you know, if we do keep seeing each other, it's likely to happen again. My dad has issues with letting go."

"He loves you, Lili. That's not an issue. Don't worry about it. It's gonna take a lot more than a gun aimed in my direction to scare me off."

"So it seems." I shake my head. "You should know his threats are not empty. Whatever you've heard or read about my family is more than likely true." Which is pretty much the same as telling him my family is involved in the criminal underground. And not just involved. They run shit.

"No one gets to choose their family, Lili. You just happen to have one that loves you, wants to protect you by any means necessary," Travis says. "Plus, if I had a daughter, there's not a chance in hell I would have let her walk away with someone like me. I mean, the things I want to do to that body of yours, Lili... Fuck..." Travis drops my hand and adjusts himself in his seat.

I want him to do all of those things to me. *Damn it, why does he have to be going out of town today?*

I pull out my phone and message Harper.

Me: Are you going to Nashville with the team?

Before I can shove it back into my purse, my cell vibrates with a response.

HARPER:

Sure am. Why?

ME:

I'm coming but don't tell anyone. I want to watch the game.

HARPER:

Okay. Who are you and what have you done with my friend? You should know, if this is a kidnapping, it's not going to end well for you…

ME:

Funny. What can I say? I have a newfound appreciation for the sport.

HARPER:

Really? Any reason in particular? Would it have anything to do with a certain player? Maybe someone with the number nine on his back?

ME:

Gotta go. I'll let you know when I'm in Nashville.

HARPER:

See you soon, babes.

I drop my phone into my bag as a new to-do list runs through my head. I need to book a flight, a hotel, find tickets. And, most importantly, I have to find a cousin to come with me because we don't travel alone. Ever. It's like an unwritten family rule.

I could ask Alessandro. My brother would probably be the safest bet. But he would also be the biggest cockblock out of everyone. Tilly, my Zio Romeo's daughter, isn't an option. She's the good girl of the family and won't go anywhere without telling the oldies what she's doing and why. Then there's Lorenzo and Enzo, my Zio Matteo's oldest sons. They're liabilities. Trouble just seems to find them wherever they go while my Zio Luca's and Zio Romeo's kids, Orlando and Dante, are too young. Which leaves me with Aurora. That's a hard no. I refuse to be responsible for that wild card. I let out a loud, irritated sigh. Alessandro it is.

Travis stops the car. "Waffle house?" I ask him while looking out the window.

"Everyone likes waffles." He shrugs.

"True."

"I can take you somewhere else?" He seems unsure of himself all of a sudden.

"Nope, this is good." I smile as I open the door

and jump out. Travis meets me in front of the car, and his hand finds mine again.

Is it normal to be comfortable with someone after such a short time? It's an odd feeling, a sense that I know him, and yet my brain is telling me I don't know a damn thing about the guy.

We sit down and a waitress is over at our table before we have a chance to pick up a menu. "Can I get you a drink to start with?" she asks, while looking directly at Travis.

"I'll have a coffee, black," he says, then turns to me. "What do you want, babe?"

"Orange juice, please," I reply, though the girl's eyes have yet to flick in my direction.

"I'll be right back with your drinks and to take your order," she says.

"Must be hard being you," I mutter to Travis.

"Why?"

"Having women put themselves out there without you even having to blink."

"Are you jealous?" He laughs. "Because if I'm not mistaken, the two guys sitting three tables to our right and one row back are giving you more than a once-over right now."

I glance at the guys in question and smile before

returning my attention to Travis. "They're probably just fans of yours." I shrug.

"Sure they are, babe." He shakes his head. "What do you feel like having?"

"Waffles," I deadpan.

"Think we are at the right place then." He chuckles.

Talking to Travis comes easy. It's not forced. I'm not sitting here trying to come up with a million things to ask him like I usually would be doing with anyone else.

"Do you get nervous before a game?"

"Not really. It's more like I get pumped. I can feel the adrenaline coursing through my veins. Being out on the ice, that's what I live for," he says. It's endearing how his face lights up whenever he talks about hockey.

"I think it's amazing that you've found something you love so much and that you get paid to do it."

"What about you? What do you do when you're not being the Valentino Princess?" he asks me with a grin, and I roll my eyes.

"I'm far from a princess. I'm in advertising. I work at Vads," I say while leaving out the part about it being one of the family's legitimate businesses.

"Beautiful and smart. You're the whole fucking package, babe. You must be creative then. Do you enjoy it? Advertising, I mean?"

"I do." I really love my job. I could be the *princess* everyone accuses me of being. I don't need to work. My trust fund is more than enough to provide for me for the rest of my life. I work because I love what I do.

The rest of breakfast breezes by with more easy conversation as we really get to know each other. It's nice.

When Travis stops in front of my parents' estate about an hour later, I jump out before he can continue up the drive. "I hope you win!"

Travis leans over the center console and calls through the open door. "Do not get out of this car without kissing me, Liliana." I don't miss the way he uses my full name.

I tuck my head back inside. "Wouldn't dream of it," I say into his mouth as our lips collide.

"I'm going to fucking miss you."

"See you soon, hotshot." I pull back and run up to the gate without looking back again.

The guard opens it for me while glaring at Travis's car like he wants to blow it up. This is exactly why I jumped out when I did. My dad's men are just as fiercely protective of me as he is, and having one gun pulled on my date is enough for today.

Chapter Ten

"O'Neil, Logan, Hines... you're starting line. Get out there. Start hard, play hard. And keep control." Those are Coach's parting words prewarm-up. Everyone stands from the benches. Bumps fists and pats backs as we make our way down the tunnel to the ice.

Away games are different from being on our home turf. When I look out into the stands, there's a sea of green and white with patches of red popping up now and then.

I skate out to the middle of the ice and focus on warming up. I don't look at the crowd as much at away games. I maneuver around the boards on our half of the rink, dribbling a puck along with me while passing it back and forth to Logan. A flash of red catches my eye, making me miss that little black disk when he slaps it in my direction. I turn my head and approach the Perspex. But it's not the color of the jersey that draws me in like a moth to a flame; it's the fiery red of her pouty fucking lips. I smile and lift a gloved hand to the window, meeting the palm she has pressed against the other side.

"What are you doing here?" I yell out over the noise of the crowd.

Lili lifts a shoulder in a half shrug. "Seems I have a sudden vested interest in hockey," she says with a huge smile curling those same lips.

My eyes flick over to the guy seated next to her, his arms crossed over his chest and his glare deadly. Alessandro. Her brother, who looks anything but impressed to be here right now. I nod my head in acknowledgement before returning my attention to Lili.

"Thank you," I tell her.

"Go and do your thing before you get in trouble," she says.

Tapping the board with my gloved fist, I skate back over to where Logan is stretching. Fall down next to him and start my own routine.

"You're either the luckiest motherfucker on the planet or a dead man walking," he grunts while shaking his head at me.

"Oh, I'm lucky all right." I grin at him. "Although I think I may have lost a fan. Her brother seems to hate my existence right now." I can still feel that death glare aimed in my direction.

"If looks could kill, eh?" Logan laughs.

After warm-ups, I make my way over to the bench while gesturing for Lili to meet me there. By the time I reach the divider that separates the tunnel from the reserved seating, she's waiting for me. Removing the glove from my right hand, I crook a finger at her. She leans in, and if I didn't have skates on, I'd climb the fucking railing. When she's close enough for me to reach out and cup her face, I fuse my lips to hers. It's a quick kiss, nothing more than a peck, but it doesn't go unnoticed by anyone looking.

"Thank you for coming," I tell her.

"As if I'd miss it." She smiles back at me.

"Wait for me? After the game?" I ask her.

Lili glances over to where her brother is seated, his eyes hyperfocused on us, and then returns her attention to me. "Okay, but I'm more than likely going to have a grumpy shadow."

"As long as I have you, I don't care who's third-wheeling." I smile and drop my arm. "See you soon, babe."

"Break a leg," she says, then quickly tries to correct herself. "Wait! Don't do that! Well, at least not one of your own. Feel free to break someone else's."

She smirks as I shake my head and make my way back to the locker room. The moment I step through the door, the whole place goes silent. All eyes aimed in my direction. While Coach pins me with a look that rivals Alessandro's when I was kissing his sister.

"What'd I miss?" I ask.

"A Valentino? Really, O'Neil? Of all the fucking pussy in New York, you had to get involved with a Valentino?" Coach sneers.

My fists curl at my sides. "Excuse me?" I do my best to even out my tone. Remain calm. Because right now, I'm ready to fucking flatten the motherfucker. Which would be career-ending, or so I've heard.

"That..." He throws an arm out towards the door. "...is going to bring nothing but trouble to this team. And I won't have it."

"I don't recall my contract stating who I could and couldn't date," I remind him before dropping my ass down on the bench in front of my locker.

"I'm telling you now."

I blink and count to five in my head. Anything to stop myself from jumping up and dropping gloves. "Yeah, that's not going to happen."

I know I've only just met the woman, but no way in hell am I going to let anyone tell me what the fuck I can and can't do. Especially when it comes to Liliana.

"This isn't fucking over. Get out there and do your damn job. We'll revisit this conversation *after* you've won this game." Coach's face is red and spittle flies out of his mouth. He's not used to hearing the word *no*.

I push up to my skates and follow my teammates down the tunnel. Then I skate out onto the ice, taking my spot on the starting line, and wait for the national anthem to play. I look over to where Lili is

kylie Kent

seated, and she waves at me with a big fucking smile on her face.

Yeah, Coach can kiss my ass if he thinks I'm giving her up.

I never thought I'd choose anything over hockey, and I'm not. Not really. Because, like I said, the team can't control who I date.

The last note dies off, and we get into position and wait for the drop. I'm blocking one of the Nashville players, who's chirping a whole bunch of nonsense. I ignore him. Which isn't hard to do. I'm still so worked up my fists are itching to hit something. The referee lifts the puck in the air, and I watch that little black disk like a hawk that hasn't seen a meal in weeks. I'm hungry for it. For the game, the adrenaline, the weight of the stick in my hand as I breeze across the ice. I have no doubt Logan will win the drop. He usually does. And I'll be ready for it.

"She's hot, ya know. And now that I know she's fair game, I'll be sure to take her for a spin, show her what it's like to fuck a winner." The son of a bitch in front of me shoves at my chest.

I look at him and then follow his line of sight. My eyes land on Lili before sweeping back again. "What the fuck did you just say, motherfucker?" I hiss out as I throw an elbow into his gut.

"I didn't stutter. I'm going to take that Valentino Princess for a spin. Tell me... is it as good as people say? Or has the shit gotten loose over time?"

The puck drops, and exactly one second later, so does my stick. Quickly followed by my gloves. My left hand wraps around his jersey while my right fist connects with his face, over and over again. I throw him off his skates, his back hits the ice, and I jump on top of him.

I get a few solid blows in before I'm pulled off by the refs and a few of my teammates. Then I'm shoved towards the Sin Bin. I don't need to hear the words. I know I just earned myself five minutes.

I look across the ice to Lili. She's staring right back at me, but I'm too far away to read her expression. The Nashville player sits on his team's bench, holding a bloody rag to his nose. I hope I fucking broke it. I hear the ref call out the penalty and I grin.

"Fucking worth it," I say right as my face is plastered on the jumbotron.

My body is fucking sore. Nashville came at me fucking hard all game. Not that I expected anything less. I gave it as good as I got it, though. And now, no amount of bruising or exhaustion is going to stop me from seeing my girl.

I walk out of the locker room and stop in my tracks. She's here, waiting for me in the hallway. "Hey." I smile at her.

"Hey yourself." Lili closes the distance as she grips my face and inspects it. I don't need to look in a mirror. I know I'm black and blue. "You should ice that," she says before slamming her lips onto mine.

"You should see the other guy." I laugh when I pull away from her mouth.

"What'd he say to you?" she asks, and I shrug.

"Nothing."

"Bullshit. You don't fight someone for no reason. What'd he say?" she tries again.

"It's hockey, babe. Fighting for no reason is exactly what we do. It's part of the game."

"Okay, I'll just go ask him myself then." She lifts a brow and attempts to pivot on her heel.

I reach out an arm and wrap it around her waist. "Yeah, you're not going anywhere near that fucker."

My eyes scan over to Alessandro, who's leaning on the far wall while pretending to ignore our conversation. His body language tells me he's heard every word, though. He pushes off and I watch him pull his phone out of his pocket and dial a number.

He says something in Italian to whoever is on the other end before holding it out to Lili. "It's Ma. She wants to know where we are."

Lili glances over her shoulder, oblivious to the fact her brother was the one to make the call in the first place. She takes the phone and quickly covers the receiver. "I'll be right back. Don't move," Lili tells me before walking farther down the hallway.

Once she's out of earshot, Alessandro turns his glare on me. "What'd he say?"

"Who?" I try to play dumb.

"The guy you laid out the second the puck dropped. Fucker said something about my sister, and I want to know what it was." It's a demand, not a question.

"Trust me, you really don't want to know," I tell him.

"I wouldn't ask if I didn't want to know," he counters. "Now, you can tell me or you can tell her. Either way, I'll find out." He shrugs as he gestures to himself, then his sister. "I'll leave it up to you to figure out which option is in your best interests."

"He said something about wanting to take her for

a spin… and he didn't mean out on the ice," I tell him through clenched teeth.

If I thought Alessandro looked pissed off before, now his blood is boiling. I can nearly see the steam coming out of his ears, his jaw so tight he's lucky if he doesn't crack a molar. "I gotta go handle something. Do me a favor and don't let her out of your sight. I'll come find her later," he says, walking off before I can respond.

Not that I would have argued with the guy. Keeping my eyes on Lili isn't a hardship.

Alessandro whispers something to Lili, takes his phone from her hand, and pockets it. She watches him go for a few seconds, then makes her way towards me while her brother storms off in the opposite direction.

"What did you tell him?"

"You ready to get out of here? You hungry? Have you eaten?" I ask instead of answering her.

"Travis, what did you tell my brother? Because I know there is no way he's leaving me alone with you without a damn good reason." She folds her arms over her chest.

"You don't want to be alone with me?" I lift a challenging brow while my lips curl into a smirk.

"Of course I do, but I want to know what has

Alessandro walking out of here looking murderous first," she says.

"That Nashville player... he said something about you I'd really rather not repeat. Your brother wanted to know what it was," I tell her.

Lili's eyes widen. "And you told him? Shit, fuck," she curses under her breath as I watch her dig her phone out of her bag.

Chapter Eleven

I dial Lorenzo's number. It almost rings out by the time he answers it. "Lil, I'm a little busy at the moment. What's up?" he asks.

"I need you to come to Nashville. Now. Alessandro is going to do something really stupid," I tell him.

"What's he doing?"

"He's going after a hockey player. You need to get here and stop him."

"The one I hear you're shacking up with? Yeah, that's probably not a good idea. I'd be more inclined to help him get rid of the body, Lil..."

"No, idiot, a different hockey player. Look, just get your ass out here and help me find him," I hiss.

"It's at least a two-hour flight. But I'll be there as soon as I can." My cousin sighs into the phone.

"Thank you." I hang up, contemplating if I should call my father next and quickly deciding against it. Because he actually *will* help Alessandro bury the body. My father has a short fuse when it comes to protecting family. An even shorter one when it comes to me.

I have no idea what that guy said before the game, but I do know it was bad enough for Travis to fight him... *and* to have my brother looking to spill some blood on his own. Without taking backup.

I glance up at Travis and catch him watching me. "I'm sorry. I have to go find my brother and stop him from killing a freaking professional athlete." That's not something we can just cover up. Especially on our own.

"If you're going, I'm going. Though something tells me your brother can handle himself, Lil."

"Oh, I know he can. But he's not thinking straight, and that's a dangerous position for the other guy to be in. I need to find Alessandro before he does something we can't undo. I do not want to be visiting my brother in a jail cell."

"Okay, come on." Travis wraps his hand around mine and tugs me forward.

I drag my feet to stop him. "You don't have to come with me. I'm sure you're tired. You should go back to your hotel."

"Not without you, I'm not."

A few quick turns later and we're walking through the back door of the arena, where there's an SUV already waiting for me. One of my brother's friends —and I use the term *friends* loosely here—opens the back door as I approach.

"Where to, Miss Valentino?" Jupe asks. The guy has worked for us for a few years now. My family trusts him.

"Where'd Alessandro go?"

Jupe's lips press into a thin line. "I don't know."

"Yes, you do. Take me wherever he went, Jupe," I say, my tone more forceful than it was a moment ago.

"Your brother wants me to take you back to the hotel."

"Well, last I checked, *my brother* is a long way off from being the boss. But if more authority is what you need, I can call Nonno? Get him to tell you himself?" It's a bitchy move, using my grandfather as a threat. But I don't have much of a choice here. It's for the greater good. The greater good being keeping my brother out of jail.

"Fine, I'll take you. I'll probably be dead the second we pull up, but I've had a good life," Jupe says, shaking his head as the door closes behind me. Travis slides in on the other side.

"Don't worry, Jupe, I'll tell 'em I held a gun to your head." I smile at him through the rearview mirror as he starts the engine.

"What gun?" Jupe asks.

I reach under the seat, knowing there are always weapons hidden in these cars. Find what I'm looking for and retrieve it from the holster that's hooked to the underside. "This one," I say cocking the gun before aiming it in Jupe's direction.

"Fuck me," Travis hisses.

I look over and realize I'm not exactly making the best impression here. Shit. I need to rein it in a bit. So I lower the gun and place it on the empty seat beside me. "Sorry."

"Don't be. That was fucking hot as shit. But let's not play with guns, Lil. I don't want you getting hurt. Or worse," Travis says, and I watch him swallow. He's really worried about me.

That doesn't stop me from rolling my eyes, though. "Because I'm a girl? I'll have you know I'm a better shot than my brother or any of my cousins— well, maybe not Aurora, but that chick is from another planet. I'm sure of it," I ramble on without meaning to.

"Not because you're a girl. Because you're *my girl*, and I want to keep you in one fucking piece," he says.

"Okay, I will only play with guns when it's really necessary," I tell him with a smile.

Travis shakes his head and laughs. "Deal."

The car pulls to a stop and my attention is drawn to the window and the bar just beyond it. "This is where he went?" I ask Jupe.

"Yep." He nods his head.

"Okay, thanks," I say as I open the back door and

climb out of the car. Travis follows me over to the sidewalk while Jupe turns off the ignition before trailing behind us.

"This is the last place I should be," Travis whispers into my ear.

I look over my shoulder at him. "Why?"

"It's Nashville's bar, Lili. This is where the team comes to celebrate... or commiserate. And tonight, we kicked their ass. They're not in a good mood," he says. "And I'm at the top of their shit list right now."

"Don't you worry your pretty little head. If anyone tries to start something with you, I'll shoot them," I deadpan.

"I actually don't know if you're joking or not, Lili... and why the fuck does that turn me on?" He lowers his lips to my ear when he says that last part.

"Because you have issues." I shrug. "And let's hope you don't have to find out if I'm joking or not," I tell him as my gaze pans over the crowded bar, looking for my brother while knowing if he's in here, he's not somewhere he can be easily seen.

I finally spot him in a darkened corner when a stray beam of light from the dance floor briefly illuminates his silhouette. "He's over here," I say under my breath as I quicken my steps in my brother's direction. I drop Travis's hand and shove against

Alessandro's chest. He doesn't move an inch. "Are you fucking crazy?" I yell and hit him again.

"What are you doing here, Lil?" he asks.

"Stopping you from doing something beyond stupid," I hiss in reply.

"Go back to the hotel. This doesn't concern you."

"Yes, it does. *You* concern me, Alessandro. I'm not having my children visit their uncle in a prison cell. Now let's go," I tell him.

My brother's eyes drop to my stomach before landing on my face again. "For the love of God, tell me you're not pregnant."

"Of course I'm not. Yet. But I will be, someday, so let's go." I tug on his arm.

He remains rooted to his corner. "I can't let this go, Lil."

"You can. You just don't want to." I peer up at him with my best doe eyes. "Please, Alessandro, take me home." I know the moment he caves.

His eyes soften and he wraps his arms around me. "I love you, Lil, and I'm not going to let anyone disrespect you. Ever. I don't give a fuck who they are," he says into my ear. I sag against his hold, refusing to let go. "Come on, let's get out of here, before I have to fight off all the fuckers currently lining up to kill your boyfriend."

"Thank you." When I turn around again, I see what Alessandro means. He wasn't being dramatic. There is literally a line of six-foot-something men blocking our path to the exit. None of them look too happy to see us standing here. Or, more accurately, to see Travis standing here.

"Fucking hell," I grumble before turning back to my brother. "Alessandro, do not let them touch him." I know Travis can hold his own. I've seen him fight. I just don't want him to have to fight. Especially because of me.

I go to move in front of him, only to be pulled up short. "Let me," Alessandro says and steps forward. "Is there a problem here?"

"Yeah, your kind ain't fucking welcome here," one of the guys spits out.

My brother's head tips to the side. "My kind?"

"Yeah, *your kind*. New Yorkers."

"I don't think I introduced myself." My brother holds out a hand. "Alessandro Valentino."

Travis and I watch on as the fucker pales in front of us while the others take a few small steps in the opposite direction. I roll my eyes for the second time tonight. "Come on, we're leaving." I take hold of Travis's hand and start pushing my way through the crowd. I know Alessandro and Jupe won't be far behind us.

I stop in my tracks when I see someone staring at me, his face already beaten to hell. Dropping Travis's hand, I walk up to the guy. "I don't know what you said on the ice today, but I hope that hurts as much as it looks like it does." I point to his black eye right as my knee comes up and connects with his balls. "You should thank me for saving your life. Next time, I won't stop my brother from hanging you from a butcher's hook," I whisper into his ear.

I step back with a smile firmly planted on my lips and take hold of Travis's hand again. I'm really not a violent person. I don't enjoy hurting other people. And usually I don't. But that doesn't mean I don't know how to do it. I am a Valentino after all, and my father made sure I was no wilting flower. He taught me to fight and to kill just as effectively as he taught my brother.

Chapter Twelve

This is a side of Lili I've never seen before. Then again, considering I've only known the woman for a few days, I'm sure there are plenty of sides of her I haven't seen yet. Honestly, she's a little scary—maybe even more so than her father and brother combined—and I sure as hell wouldn't want to be on her shit list.

How can someone so sweet and fucking pure also carry that level of brutality and aggression with her?

I don't know. But watching her knee that asshole in the balls was something else. I'm conflicted, torn between wanting to shove her behind me and not let anyone get to her... and wanting to see just what she's capable of.

I follow her out of the bar, her brother and their friend trailing behind us. Lili opens the door of the SUV that's still parked at the curb and climbs inside. As soon as my ass lands on the seat beside her, she turns to me. "I'm really sorry. I swear I'm not usually like this. But I'd get it if you wanted me to just drop you at your hotel and part ways now."

"My hotel room is fine... *if* you're planning on coming with me. If not, I'll follow you wherever you're going, babe," I tell her. "And you can be yourself, Lili. Whatever that means, no matter how many versions there are. I want to get to know you, the real you. Not the you that you think I want to see."

"Okay," she whispers with a small smile. It drops the moment the doors open again and her brother and friend get inside the car.

Lili reaches over and grabs hold of my hand. I have no idea where we're going, and I don't ask, because I meant what I said. I'm going wherever she's going. Usually, I'd be out with my team. Especially after a win. Tonight, there's only one way I want to celebrate, and that's with the woman sitting next to me. Preferably naked.

A few minutes later, we're pulling into a garage under an apartment building. "This is one of my Zio Luca's places. We're kind of borrowing it," Lili explains.

"Kind of?" I ask.

"Well, we didn't exactly tell anyone where we were going," she says.

"Why not?"

"Because I didn't want my father to ground the jet." She shrugs. "He's not exactly a fan of yours right now, and trust me when I say he will do anything and everything to keep me from seeing you."

I've been wanting to ask her what her father said to her when we ran into him the other day. I know it's really none of my business, though.

"Not a fan is an understatement, Lil. I've never seen Pops want to gut someone as much as he wants to gut you." Alessandro looks over to me while pressing the button for the elevator.

"Shut it," Lili hisses at her brother.

"What? It's the truth." He smirks.

"He's not going to gut you," Lili attempts to clarify. "He might want to, but he won't."

I don't say anything. My head is spinning with all of this talk about her father... and being at the top of his very real hit list.

How the fuck did this become my life overnight?

I look at Lili and squeeze her hand tighter. That's how. She's got some kind of spell over me, because I can't for the life of me find a reason to let her go, even knowing all the dangers that come with us being together.

Lili drags me down a hallway in her uncle's apartment, and Alessandro calls out after us, "Door stays open, Lil."

"You wish," she throws back. And as soon as we step foot in the room, she makes a point of slamming the door shut. "We're only staying here until my cousin shows up. Then we can leave," she says. "I just need to make sure someone is here to stop my brother from going after that douchebag again."

"You think he'd go back?" I ask her.

"I know he's already planning it." She nods. "Trust me, he won't let it go. But once Lorenzo gets here, my brother is his problem. And you and I... well, we can get to the celebrating part of the night."

"Yeah? What'd you have in mind?" I ask while taking a step forward. She takes one back. We repeat the process until the undersides of her knees are hitting the edge of the bed.

"Well, I thought we could go to a hotel."

"And what would we do at this hotel, Lili?" I run the tips of my fingers along her neck, and she tilts her head to one side, allowing my lips to dip down and replace my hand.

"We'd, uh... well... fuck..." She gasps when I bite down.

"Mmm, I like your kind of celebrating," I hum. "How long before your cousin gets here? Because I gotta tell you, you've had my cock hard all fucking night, babe."

"Um... maybe we could start the celebrations early," she says as she reaches a hand down and cups my cock over the denim of my jeans.

A loud bang has her dropping that hand like I've

burned her. The door swings open, and I take a step back. Not because I want to, but because I'm trying to be respectful. To her. And to her family.

"That ain't fucking happening on my watch, Lil," Alessandro grunts, one arm outstretched as he points a finger from me to his sister.

At least it's not a gun, I think to myself.

"Oh my god." Lili throws her hands in the air. "You're being ridiculous, Alessandro. You know I'm an adult, right? That I've had sex plenty of times before and will have it plenty more."

I look at her. It's on the tip of my tongue to ask for their names. I don't like the idea of other guys knowing what she feels like. I'm not an idiot. I know she wasn't a virgin. But, fuck, hearing her talk about fucking other guys doesn't sit well with me.

"Got a list?" I ask, not able to stop myself.

"A list?" Lili turns to me.

"Of these guys. The ones you've had *plenty of sex* with," I clarify.

"No, and what makes you think they're all guys?" She raises a questioning brow at me.

"Babe, I couldn't care less about their gender. I just want them gone," I tell her.

Lili rolls her eyes at me. "Fine, I'll give you my list... as soon as you give me yours." She smirks.

"As entertaining as this *isn't*, the fucking door stays open," Alessandro grunts. "Unless you'd like a bullet between your boyfriend's eyes."

"I'm telling Mom," Lili says.

"Tell her. I'll tell Pops why I had to follow your ass to fucking Nashville," he counters.

I'm an only child, so this whole *sibling rivalry* thing is something I've never understood. I can't help but smile as I watch them try to one-up each other, though.

"Anyone hungry? I'm going to order takeout," I say while pulling my phone from my pocket.

Alessandro and Lili both look at me with odd expressions on their faces.

"What?"

"Nothing," they say at the same time.

Chapter Thirteen

I thought I would never get out of that apartment. When my cousin Lorenzo finally turned up, I took my opportunity to leave. Told my brother and cousin I'd see them in the morning. Neither of them appreciated my decision. They both tried to force me to stay, to the point they threatened Travis with bodily harm.

Which left me to wonder if he has some kind of death wish or if nothing really fazes him. He's the only guy who's been willing to stick around after meeting my family. We did get out, though. I might have had to use calling our Nonna as leverage—we all knew she would have put Alessandro and Lorenzo in their place. Either way, the result was the same. They relented and let us leave.

Next time I want to go out of town to watch Travis play, I'm taking one of my female cousins with me. That's if there even is a next time after all the craziness that's happened tonight.

The moment the door to his hotel suite closes behind me, all thoughts of my family disappear. Because this is what I've been waiting for all night. Getting him alone and naked and having him deliver on that pleasure he's so good at.

I practically jump him. My legs wrap around his waist and my arms lock over his neck. Travis's hands cup my ass, taking on my full weight like it's nothing before he presses me up against the closest wall.

"I need you," I say into his mouth between hurried, hungry kisses.

"Not half as much as I need you." Travis grinds

his cock against my pussy, proving just how much he means it. Then he spins around and starts walking us through the suite.

I don't notice I'm falling until my back hits the top of the bed and Travis's body follows me. His hand moves up underneath my jersey, *his* jersey, cupping my breast over the lace of my bra.

"Fuck, I need to see you." Travis pushes himself up and pulls the jersey over my head; then he reaches behind my back and unclasps my bra. The material flutters to the floor as his fingers flick the button on my jeans, and he removes each shoe one by one before sliding my jeans and panties down my thighs. "Next time you come to a game, wear a skirt," he says.

My brows furrow as I peer up at him. "Why?"

"Because I want easier access to *this*," he says while running his fingers through my wet folds.

"Oh, shit," I hiss out as my hips lift off the bed. I'm completely naked now, and he's... not. Which is something I need to rectify. Immediately.

I move up on my knees and lift the hem of his shirt. Travis tugs it the rest of the way over his head while my eyes take in all of him. Every hard inch of muscle. My fingers trace over a big ugly bruise on his ribs.

"Does this hurt?" I ask as I lean forward to press a gentle kiss to the discolored skin.

"No." Travis tells me. "But my cock does. Wanna kiss that better too?" He smirks at me.

I slide off the bed. His eyes follow my every movement as I drop to my knees. He pivots his body so that his legs hang off the edge of the mattress. And I have to admit that the look he's giving me right now is that much more of a turn-on.

"Take them off," I say while pointing to his pants.

"Fuck, you're the hottest fucking thing I've ever laid eyes on, Lili," he groans before removing his pants. His cock springs free and bounces up against his lower abdomen.

Crawling forward, I position myself between his spread legs. My hand wraps around his cock, and my lips lightly kiss the tip.

Travis hisses as his hand cups my cheek. "Suck me."

My pussy gushes at his words. I don't know if it's the thought of having him in my mouth, or his commanding tone that does it for me. But I'm not going to question it, because I want him. I want to please him. I want to be whatever he needs right now.

Licking my lips, I close my mouth around his tip, just the tip, and suck. I keep my eyes on his face as I slowly lower myself down on his shaft as far as I can go without choking.

"Fuck. Yes. Just like that, babe. Take me. It's all yours," Travis praises, and I get a different kind of warm sensation in my stomach.

The idea that this man is mine, just mine... I like it. I've never wanted anyone to be mine more than I do with him. Maybe I've been dick-matized. Because wanting to be his, needing him to be mine after just a couple of days, is absurd.

Though this is not the time to question my sanity or the reasons I feel the way I do. That's tomorrow's problem.

Flattening my tongue on the underside of his cock, I slide up his length, to the tip, before my head bobs back down again. I reach a hand towards my pussy. My clit is throbbing, begging to be touched as I press my fingers down and sigh when the pleasure builds between my thighs. My hips thrust forward, grinding against my palm as I continue to suck on Travis's cock.

"Fuck me, I want you to make yourself come while my cock is jammed down your pretty little throat," he says before wrapping a hand around my hair. Then he starts guiding my movements, thrusting up into my mouth at a faster pace.

I moan around him, my fingers matching his rhythm as they rub at my clit. I can feel my orgasm building. I'm so close.

"Fuck yes. I'm going to come, Lili," Travis warns. I don't pull away. I want him. I want his taste on my tongue.

The moment the first squirt hits the back of my throat, I fall over the edge. And my own orgasm hits me like a freight train. Crashing into me. Leaving me heaving as I pull back from his cock. Travis reaches down and picks me up from the floor. My legs settle on each side of his hips, and his lips slam down on mine before his tongue pushes into my mouth.

My hand flies out, swatting at whatever's touching my face. "Ow, shit, you do not hit like a girl, babe," Travis grunts.

My eyes snap open. "Travis?" Then flick around the room while memories of last night creep into my consciousness. "What time is it?"

"It's five thirty," he says.

"In the afternoon? Why didn't you wake me?"

"No, in the morning." He chuckles. "I have to go."

"You're leaving? Now? It's not even daytime yet." I squeeze my eyes shut again.

"Sorry. I didn't want to leave without saying goodbye." His lips press to mine and I can't help but smile against them.

"Mmm. Where are you going?"

"We have a game in Vegas. I'll be back to New York in a few days," he says.

"Okay." I sigh. As much as I want to follow him, I know I can't. I have to go home. I might work for my family's company but I still *work*. And I have a job to do.

"I'll see you in a few days," Travis tells me.

"I'm getting up," I reply, even though my eyes are still closed.

"Don't. Stay here and sleep. Just drop the key off at the desk before you leave."

"Okay. Try to not miss me too much while you're off in Vegas with all those showgirls." I yawn.

"They ain't got nothing on you, babe. See you soon."

"Lil, where are you?" Alessandro's voice blares against my eardrum.

"I'm sleeping. Why?" I ask him.

"I didn't ask what you were doing. I asked you where you were. We gotta go home. Pops is losing his mind. So where the hell are you? I'm coming to get you," he says.

I groan into the phone. "I'm at the Four Seasons. I'll meet you outside," I tell him before hanging up and dragging myself out of bed.

I head straight for the bathroom, shower as quickly as I can, and then get dressed. I pick up my phone and bag and walk out. Dropping the keycard in the check-out box on my way through the lobby. I manage to get to the front of the hotel before my brother pulls up. Tapping the screen of my phone while I wait for him, I open the missed messages.

TRAVIS:

Miss you already. Let me know when you get home.

A stupid smile spreads across my face as I tap out

a reply and pocket my phone right as Alessandro
pulls up in front of me.

> ME:
>
> On my way to the jet now. Think of
> me when you're jerking off tonight.

My phone vibrates but I don't have time to check
the notification. Instead, I drop the device into my
bag and climb into the back of the car.

"Why is Pops losing his mind?" I ask Alessandro
as soon as I slam the door shut behind me.

"Because he hasn't laid eyes on his pride and joy
for the last twenty-four hours."

I roll my eyes. "I really need to move out."

"Good luck with that." This comes from beside
me, where my cousin Lorenzo is seated with a stupid
smirk plastered on his face. "There is no way in hell
Zio Theo is letting you leave that house."

"I'm an adult. I can do what I want," I'm quick to
remind him.

"Mhmm, let me know how that works for you."
Alessandro laughs from the driver's seat.

"I hate you both," I mutter under my breath
while staring out the window. "I'll discuss it with
Mom first. Once she's on board with it, she'll make

sure Dad doesn't blow a gasket when I bring it up to him."

My parents love hard. My brother and I are their world. Which makes it difficult for them to let go— my father more so than my mother. If he could, he would literally have me locked in a room where no one could access me. I'm not complaining. I've grown up surrounded by love, but there are times that it can all be very... suffocating.

My phone vibrates again in my bag so I pull it out and navigate to my unread messages.

TRAVIS:

> Fuck, Lili, you can't say shit like that to me when I'm a million miles away from you. Now I have a hard-on, sitting on a jet surrounded by my teammates.

TRAVIS:

> Don't touch yourself. When I get back into town, I want you weeping and ready for me.

TRAVIS:

> Already counting down the minutes till I can slide into you again.

ME:

> Is now a good time to tell you my father probably has my phone cloned and likely reads my messages?

TRAVIS:

> Shit? Really?

TRAVIS:

> Fuck it. He already wants to kill me. It'll be worth it. You're worth it.

ME:

> I think that might be the sweetest thing anyone has ever said to me.

TRAVIS:

> See you soon, babe.

"Fucking hell, Lil. Why do you have to look so happy?" Alessandro asks while glancing back at me.

And it's only now that I realize Lorenzo's nosey ass has been reading my entire conversation. "She's texting lover boy."

"It's hard to kill someone who makes you look like that, sis," my brother grumbles, and I narrow my glare on the back of his head.

"You're not touching him."

"I don't like the guy," Alessandro says. "He's far too cocky."

"Compared to all of you?" I gesture from my brother to my cousin. "Besides, Dad promised none of you would hurt him."

"How the hell did you get him to agree to that?"

"I just told him the truth. That I really like Travis—like *really, really* like him. And if anything were to happen to him, it'd make me cry. A lot." I smile. My father cannot stand to see me cry. Nothing sends him into more of a murderous rage than seeing me upset.

Did I use that knowledge to get whatever I wanted when I was younger? Yes. It would have been stupid not to. Am I using it now to stop him from going after my boyfriend? Again, yes. For the same reason.

I don't care what that says about me. Because what I told my father was the truth. I do really, really like Travis. And I want to see where this relationship goes. I've never met anyone like him before. I've never felt this comfortable with anyone before. It's this sense I get whenever he looks at me. Like he understands and sees me.

For the first time in my life, I feel *seen*. Which is odd, considering I'm used to having all eyes on me all the time.

Chapter Fourteen

The moment I step off the jet, I pull my phone out of my pocket. For the last three days, I've been texting back and forth with Lili. We've been talking about everything and anything. I've been purposely thinking of random questions to ask her just to give her a reason to reply.

I really like this chick. I don't want to talk to anyone else but her. I'm supposed to be going to see my parents today; instead, I've asked Lili to meet me at my place. I sent my mother a message, making up some bullshit excuse about being tired and telling her I'd catch up with them tomorrow. Right now, I just want to see my girl.

Except, when I walk into my apartment, it's not her who I find waiting for me. It's her father.

"Where's Lili? Is she okay?" I drop my bag, barely registering the sound it makes when it hits the floor. I should be wondering why he's standing here, how he got in. Fuck, I should probably be looking for the closest exit. But the first thing that comes to mind isn't my own safety or well-being. It's Lili's.

Her father is standing in my foyer, his hands in his pockets and his head slightly tilted. Assessing me. "She's fine," he finally says, and I exhale my relief.

"Want a drink?" I offer before walking past him and farther into my apartment.

"No."

"Okay," I say and turn back around to face him. "I'm assuming there's a reason for your visit. I don't get the impression you make house calls to all of your daughter's friends."

"Friends? Is that what you are? *Friends?*" he asks.

I take a second to consider his question. Lili might be the first girl I've actually enjoyed getting to know. Does that make us friends? Sure, but it's more than that too.

"We're friends," I tell him. "Without friendship, there isn't much of a relationship, is there?"

"My daughter likes you, Mr. O'Neil," he says.

"And I like her."

"What exactly are your intentions with Liliana?" He doesn't move a muscle, and there's no hint of emotion on his face. I have to remember never to play poker with this guy. He gives nothing away.

"I want to get to know her. I don't have anything but good intentions when it comes to Lili." I have no idea what her father wants to hear, what the right thing to say is. I also have no idea how much I should put my cards on the table. I don't think saying I intend to keep her as mine is going to go over too well with a guy who's used to maintaining control.

"You know who our family is?"

"I've become aware."

"And you're not worried?" Mr. Valentino's lips tip up slightly with the question, like he finds it amusing.

I shrug. "She's worth whatever bullshit comes my way."

"*That* is something we can agree on," he says. "You should know... if you do anything to hurt her, if she so much as sheds a single fucking tear because of you, I'll enjoy tearing you apart bit by bit. And I do mean literally." He pins me with a hard glare before adding, "Do you know how long someone can be kept alive while their body is cut to pieces? Because I do. Down to the second."

"I have no intentions of hurting her, sir," I tell him.

"Good. And this..." He gestures between us. "Never happened. I was never here."

"Noted." I nod my head and watch as the scariest fucking man I've ever met walks out the door, clicking it closed behind him.

I take a breath, grab my bag, and carry it into my bedroom. Checking the time as I go. I'm anxious to see Lili. Her family can continue to dish out threats. It doesn't stop me from wanting her.

When there's a knock on my door a few minutes later, I walk back out to the foyer and open it. My arm snakes around Lili's waist, pulling her inside, and my lips slam onto hers. "Fuck, I missed you," I say into her mouth before pushing my tongue inside.

"Mmm, I missed you more." She smiles against

the kiss. When she pulls away, she looks me up and down. "What he say to you?"

"Who?"

"My father. I know he was here. So what'd he say?"

"How do you know he was here?"

"I ran into him downstairs, and he looked like he'd just been caught sticking his hand into the cookie jar. What'd he say?" she asks again.

"Nothing much." I shrug. "I want to take you out. To dinner. But, fuck, I really want to fuck you too." I step back and really look at her. She's wearing a tight little pencil skirt and a light-pink blouse that shows me the outline of her bra. "That's how you dress at the office?" I shake my head. "Damn, if this hockey thing doesn't pan out, I need to come work for you, babe."

Lili laughs. "I think the hockey thing is working out just fine for you. So dinner? Where are you thinking?"

"Anywhere you want?"

"Mmm, do you like Italian?"

"I like eating you. You're Italian." I smirk.

"I'm also Russian." She laughs.

"So fucking hot." My hands find her waist again and I tug her forward.

"We can order in," she says. "Eat naked, in bed, between orgasms."

"That sounds like a great fucking idea, but you deserve better than that. Come on, let's go." I grab Lili's hand and open the door before I'm tempted to take her up on her offer.

Lili sits across from me as her eyes bounce around the restaurant's interior. "Have you eaten here before?" she asks me.

"No, but I've heard it's good. Have you?"

"A lot. My family owns it," she says.

"So I'm guessing the food's good?"

"Very." Lili nods.

"Then why do you look like you'd rather be anywhere else?" I lift a questioning brow before adding, "We *can* go somewhere else. I don't mind."

"No, I like the food. And we're here so we may as well stay. I just... My family can be insane, as you've seen, and I don't want anyone jumping out of the shadows and scaring you off."

"Babe, I already told you I don't scare off so

easily. And your family loves you. That's not something you need to apologize for," I remind her.

"What's your family like? What was it like growing up as an only child?"

"Lonely, but my parents are great. The typical middle-class family." I lift a shoulder. There really isn't much to tell.

"You were lonely?"

"It comes with being an only child. That's why when we have kids, we're making our own hockey team of boys."

"I'm not breeding a hockey team, and I don't think that's the way biology works. You can't just proclaim you're having boys."

"That's not a *no* to having my babies." I smile at her, and she shrugs.

"What can I say? You'd make stupidly good-looking babies."

"Nice to know you like me for my personality." I laugh.

"I think you're the complete package," she says. "By the way, I heard something yesterday."

"You heard something? What'd you hear?" I ask her.

"That you're a free agent and other teams are looking to acquire you."

"I am."

"So if another team snaps you up—because, let's be honest, you're good and someone is going to want you—you'll have to leave New York," she says.

"Something like that is months away, Lili. But now that you mention it, what are your thoughts on Canada?"

"The country?" she attempts to clarify.

"Yes, the country." I laugh.

"It's... Canada."

"Would you live there?"

"Are you telling me you're moving to Canada?" She narrows her glare at me.

"I could be. I mean, I've wanted to play for the Knights my entire life, and my people have been in discussions with them," I tell her. "If I move to Vancouver, I'm going to want to take you with me."

"Vancouver?" she parrots as her eyes widen.

"You don't like Vancouver?"

"No, I do. It's just... Never mind. Are you really asking me if I'd move to a whole different country with you?"

"Yes."

"But we barely know each other."

"We know each other plenty," I tell her.

"But to live together? That's a big call," Lili says.

"Let's give it a trial run then. Move in with me here. See if you like it." I grin, and she laughs.

"You really do have a death wish."

"I have a *being with you* wish, babe."

"Mmm, how about we start with baby steps? I'll leave a toothbrush at your place."

"I'll take it. But the offer still stands. If I'm home, I want you there with me, Lili. Scratch that. I want you there even when I'm not. I like knowing you're at my place. In my bed."

"I was thinking of getting my own apartment," she says, instead of answering me.

"Why? Mine's big enough for both of us."

"Because, one, I want to keep you in one piece. And, two, I've never lived on my own, and I want to know what that feels like before moving in with someone else."

"Okay. Well, there are plenty of available units in my building, and I've heard you have connections with the owners, so maybe you should look there first," I suggest.

"You're not used to *not* getting your way, are you?"

"No. I'm an only child, remember?"

"Well, now's a good time to start." Lili laughs,

and as much as I hate that she's turning down my offer, I also admire her independence.

Chapter Fifteen

Two months. I've been dating Travis for two months. It's been intense. The feelings I have for him grow deeper and deeper every day. I miss him so much when he's away. I've been flying in to as many games as I can. I'm now a regular at the home games. Along with my brother and cousins. I refuse to sit in the box with them, though. Instead, I stay right near the bench. Where I can see Travis close up.

There's something insanely hot about watching him play hockey. He has a passion for the game like nothing I've ever seen before. Well, that's a lie. He's really passionate about my body too, and bringing it all kinds of pleasure.

"You okay?" Travis's hand reaches over and wraps around mine, pulling me out of my thoughts.

"Uh-huh, just nervous. What if they don't like me?" I ask him.

"They're going to love you. I mean, really, what's not to love?" He grins down at me.

Love. We haven't uttered those words to each other yet. Am I in love with Travis? Yes, I am, but I'm not a crazy person, and I'm not about to tell him that. Not until he tells me first at least.

"I just... I don't want to embarrass you or anything."

"You could never embarrass me, babe. You are perfection and anyone who doesn't think that can go and fuck right off," he says.

I smile. "Thank you."

Travis uses his free hand to push inside the house. *His parents'* house. It's a nice home. Two stories, white siding with blue shutters. And the complete opposite of how I grew up. There are no armed guards, no cameras following our movements, no one scrutinizing what we're doing at every turn.

"You've met my mother. And trust me, babe, she already loves you."

"I met her once. The morning after we fucked, not the best first impression," I hiss under my breath.

"Ma, Dad, you here?" Travis ignores my comments as he yells out through the house.

"In here," a female voice calls back.

Travis leads me into the kitchen and throws out an arm towards his mother. "Ma, this is Liliana. Lili, my mom, Frances."

Mrs. O'Neil wipes her hands on a tea towel before stepping up to us. "I know who she is, Travis. We've met." She glares at her son before turning to me. "How are you, sweetheart? It's so good to see you again. I've been bugging Travis to bring you around."

"I'm good. Thank you for having me. You have a lovely home, Mrs. O'Neil," I say as she pulls me in for a hug.

"It's just Frances." She releases me with a smile, then looks over to Travis again. "Your father's by the grill. You two can go on out. I'll be there in a sec."

"Do you need a hand with anything?" I offer.

"Oh, no, sweetheart. You're our guests. Travis, get the girl a drink," she says before waving us off.

"Come on, babe." Travis guides me through a sliding glass door and out onto a deck. "Dad, you grilling or cremating those steaks?" he calls out to his father in a teasing tone.

A middle-aged man, who appears to be a carbon copy of Travis only older, turns around with a huge smile on his face. He sets a pair of tongs aside and walks over to us. "You must be Liliana. My son hasn't stopped talking about you. I'm Sean. It's so good to finally meet you."

"You too," I tell him and can feel the blush creeping up my cheeks.

"Dad, do not embarrass me. She still thinks I'm cool," Travis grumbles.

I look at his father and shake my head. "I let him think that, but I've seen his collection of Star Wars figurines. The cool factor went way down the moment I saw those." I laugh.

"Oh, I like you. Come on, have a seat. What can I get you to drink?" Mr. O'Neil asks.

139

"Your parents are really nice," I tell Travis on the ride home. "Normal."

"As opposed to what?" He laughs. "Were you expecting aliens or something?"

"No, but you've met my family. Some of them. And they're certainly not normal," I remind him.

"Your family is fine," he says.

"Really?" I ask with raised brows. "Okay, let's do this."

"Do what?"

"Go to my place. My parents' house," I say. I haven't taken Travis home yet. I haven't wanted to scare him. He's dropped me off at the gate plenty of times. But I've never invited him inside.

"Okay," he says, seemingly unfazed.

"Just, um, whatever you see at my house, you didn't see it." I pull out my phone and send my mother a quick text.

ME:

> Mom, I'm bringing Travis over. Do me a favor and send Dad out on an errand or something.

MOM:

> He's already out. But you know he'll find out you have a guest the moment you drive through the gates.

ME:

Can we at least pretend to be as normal as possible for an hour? Just an hour.

MOM:

We are normal, Lil.

I tuck my phone away again. I don't bother arguing with my mother. She knows we're not normal. Despite being mafia royalty, she didn't grow up in this world. Her parents were from warring families—some real-life *Romeo and Juliet* type shit. They ran off together and raised my mom and my Zia Lilah under aliases. So as much as she gets it, she also doesn't. She tries her best though.

When Travis pulls up to the gate, I instruct the guard to let us through, speaking in Italian while pleading with him to wait fifteen minutes before calling my father. I know he won't. My father's men are loyal to a fault. As they should be.

"You can park over there." I point to the side of the driveway, and Travis pulls us into the open spot.

"You look more nervous here than you were meeting my parents."

"I just don't want you to leave me," I admit.

He turns in the driver's seat to look at me, reaching out a hand to tip my chin up and force me to look at him too. "Lili, I promise I'm not leaving you."

"Okay..." I sigh. "When we go in, they're going to want to search you. It's protocol. I'm sorry."

"It's fine. Come on, show me this palace you grew up in. I can't wait to see pictures of you as a kid. I bet you never even had an awkward teenage phase." Travis laughs.

I take his hand and lead him through the front door. We make it two steps inside before three men stop us. "Miss Valentino." They nod at me.

"This is my friend, Travis," I say, waving a hand between them. "Travis, this is John, Michael, and Chris."

"Good game last night," Chris says, a slight smile spreading his lips before his professionalism snaps back in place. "We need to search you, Mr. O'Neil. Please hold out your arms."

Travis does as he's instructed while Chris pats him down.

"Okay, that's enough. He's a hockey player, not an assassin," I grind out, tug on Travis's hand, and lead him through the massive foyer. I can't help but wonder what it's like to see this place from his point of view. I grew up like this and have never known anything different.

I stop short when we approach one of the living rooms and curse under my breath. I knew I shouldn't have told my mother we were coming.

"Mom?" I question as my eyes scan the room full of people. Not just people, *family*. All of my aunts are here. Nonna too. "What's going on?"

"Oh my god! No wonder you've been keeping him hidden away," My Zia Savvy says before letting out a low whistle. "Damn, Lil, you did good."

"Kill me now," I grumble as I cover my face with my hands.

"Sorry, Lil, I swear I only told her," Mom says while hitching a thumb towards my aunt. "She was already here."

"Travis, this is my mom, Maddie. Mom, Travis." I do my best to force down my embarrassment as I make introductions.

"It's a pleasure to meet you, Mrs. Valentino," Travis says.

"You can call me Maddie," Mom corrects while tugging Travis into her arms. My mom's a big hugger.

"This is my nonna, Holly," I explain and then move on to my aunts.

"You're staying for dinner, right, Travis? I've already told the kitchen staff to prepare a feast," Mom says more than asks.

"We can't stay, Mom. Travis has... things to do." I try to come up with a quick excuse and fall short.

"We can stay, babe," Travis interjects. "Thank you, Mrs. Valentino. I'd love to stay for dinner."

"Great." My mother beams at him.

"What the fuck is going on in here?"

The sound of my father's voice booming from the doorway has everyone turning in his direction. And I immediately jump in front of Travis. I don't think my dad will shoot him, not in a room full of women, but I also wouldn't put it past him to forget he has an audience.

"Theo, language," Nonna scolds.

"Sorry, Ma," Dad replies before turning to my mother. "Maddie, you didn't tell me we were having a party?"

"I didn't know I needed your permission," Mom fires back.

"What are we celebrating?" This comes from my Zio Romeo, who walks up behind my father.

"Lil has a boyfriend," his wife, my Zia Livvy, tells him.

"Does she now?" He takes Travis in from head to toe, likely envisioning all the ways he and the rest of my uncles could dismember the guy.

The whole time, I haven't taken my eyes off my

father. I walk over and wrap my arms around his waist. "Dad, please, for once, just be nice. For me," I whisper.

"I'm always nice to you, Liliana," he says.

"To Travis. Be nice to Travis," I huff.

"He's not good enough for you," Dad grunts.

"No one is. But we can pretend your standards aren't ridiculous for one night," I try again. "Because I happen to really like him." I drop my arms and give my dad my best puppy-dog eyes before moving over to greet my uncle, right as his twin strolls into the room.

"Who died?" My Zio Luca asks, his hands in his pockets as he rocks on his heels.

"No one. Yet," Dad tells him.

"Theo, a word," Mom says in that no-nonsense tone she has when she wants to make a point. I know she's going to read him the riot act and warn him to be on his best behavior.

"Lil brought a guy home, Luc," Zio Romeo says.

"Shit. Really? Fuck, Lil. Why are you doing this to us? When did you even start dating? And who the fuck let that happen on their watch?" Zio Luca rambles while raking an exasperated hand through his hair.

"Funny. You do know I'm an adult, right? Travis is not my first boyfriend," I tell him.

"I'm going to pretend I didn't hear that," my uncle says to me as he walks up to Travis with an outstretched hand. "I'm Luca. I'll be the one holding you down while my brother skins you alive—ya know, if you make the dumbass mistake of hurting my niece."

"Travis, and that won't happen, sir. I might not be Lili's first boyfriend, but I will be her last."

Chapter Sixteen

I f you've ever wanted to be on an episode of *The Sopranos,* having dinner at Lili's house will satisfy any curiosity you ever had about the inner workings of a mafia family.

Lili was on edge all night, and I hated it. I don't like seeing her so stressed out or anxious. Her childhood home should be the place where she's most relaxed. It was clear she wasn't worried about herself, though; she was worried about me. *For me.*

"I think you should come home with me. You're wound tight, babe, and I happen to know the best way to help you relax," I tell Lili.

She walked me out to my car and then decided to tell me she was staying behind tonight. "I'm sure you could. I'll come by later, but I need to talk to my mom first. I'll drive over in a bit," she says.

"You sure? I don't mind waiting for you." I wrap my arms around her waist and pull her against me.

Lily leans up on her tiptoes. Her lips brush against mine. "I'm sure. See you soon. Maybe drink one of those pre-workout shakes you have. You'll need all the energy you can muster up, hotshot."

"I'll never run out of energy for you, babe. Don't make me wait too long or I might have to start without you," I tell her with a grin.

"I'm about to go talk to my mother, and now I have the image of you jerking off in my head. Thanks for that." Lily shoves at my chest before turning and walking back towards the house.

It's been two hours. What could possibly be taking her so damn long?

I pick up my phone for the tenth time. Lili hasn't responded to my last four messages. I press the call button next to her name. It rings out and her voice-mail picks up.

"You've reached Liliana Valentino. Please leave a message and I'll get back to you at my earliest convenience."

"Lili, call me back... or text me. Let me know you're okay." I sigh into the phone, then add, "Please," before hanging up. My phone lands on the sofa at the same time the door to my apartment opens. "Lili?" I call out while making my way to the foyer.

"Well, you better not be expecting anyone else for a booty call, Travis. I never did learn to share well," she says, appearing in front of me.

"You okay?" I ask as I inspect every inch of her face. Her eyes are red and puffy. She's been crying.

"Uh-huh. Sorry it took me so long." Lili forces a smile on her face.

"Who made you cry, Liliana?" My fists are clenching at my sides. The need to hurt whoever created those tears is strong.

"It's nothing. Now, come on. Show me that unending energy you promised me." She removes her coat and lays it over the sofa.

"Lili, you crying is not nothing. I want to know why," I tell her.

"It's really not a big deal. I'm just tired, and when I'm tired, I get teary-eyed," she says.

"Humor me then. What made you cry?" I wrap my arms around her tighter. Pick her up and walk us over to the sofa. Where I sit down before placing her legs on each side of my thighs.

"I have to go to Italy for a month with my family," she blurts out.

I blink at her. "Babe, most people don't cry over having to spend a month in Italy." My fingers wipe the stray tears that fall down her cheeks.

"It's not Italy that's the problem. It's... the whole month that I won't be able to see you, Travis. I don't think I want to go a whole month without seeing you," she says.

"Lili, there are things called jets, phones, video chats. I promise you, wherever you are in the world, you will never have to go a whole month without seeing me. Because I couldn't fathom not being able to see you for that long either."

"I'm sorry," she says.

"For what?"

"For my family. For the way they're treating you. For having to leave for a month. It was my Nonna's idea and, well, my grandfather makes sure she gets whatever she wants. But I also think..." Her voice dies off.

"You think what?" I press her.

"I think there's about to be some—how do I say this? Um, company restructuring going on in the family," she says.

"Meaning your dad's taking over for your grandfather?"

"Something like that." She shrugs. "I think so at least. It's weird... for all of us to be going to Italy right now."

"It's only a month. It'll fly by, babe. And I promise you'll see me so much you're going to get tired of looking at this face." I gesture a circle around my head for emphasis.

"Impossible," she says, leaning forward and melding her lips with mine.

I pick her up and take her into my bedroom, gently placing her in the middle of the bed. Lifting her right leg, I remove her heel before doing the same with the left side. I want to take my time, slowly unwrap this woman like it's Christmas morning. I grab hold of Lili's hips and flip her body over so she's lying on her stomach.

"Shit, warn a girl next time," she squeals.

My palm lands on her ass. "Shh, you're ruining my gift," I tell her.

"Your gift?" she asks, while looking over her shoulder at me.

"You, babe, are the best goddamn gift I've ever received. And, right now, I'm trying to enjoy unwrapping you."

"Well, don't let me interrupt you then." Lili lowers her head to the mattress.

My fingers pinch the zipper of her dress, slowly pulling it down the middle of her back. Exposing her smooth, tanned skin. Inch by inch. When I reach the bottom, I flip Lili over again and slide the straps along her arms.

"Fuck me, I think God sent me an angel I didn't deserve when you fell from heaven."

"Well, it's a damn good thing you caught me then." Lili smiles.

"Quick reflexes, babe. We can thank years of

hockey practice for that," I tell her as I continue to glide the material of her dress down her body.

"Travis?"

"Yeah, babe?" I ask as the fabric pools around her ankles.

"Less talking and more enjoying." Lili waves a hand down her body.

"Oh, I appreciate it plenty. So fucking much." My fingers hook into the sides of her panties and I drag them along the length of her legs. Once she's left completely bare on the bed, I push to my feet and look down at her. Reaching behind my neck, I tug my shirt over my head and then kick off my pants before I open a drawer, pull out a string of condoms, and place them on the bed.

"Someone's ambitious tonight," Lili says with a raised brow.

I don't respond to her with words. Instead, I cover her body with mine, my mouth closes over one of her nipples, and my fingers tweak its pair. Sucking then nibbling. I bite down harder when she moans and her chest lifts off the mattress. I move lower. I need to taste her. I had every intention of going slow. Worshiping every bit of her flesh. But now I'm starved. I position my shoulders between her thighs, and my tongue darts out to lick right up the center of her folds. Her taste explodes in my mouth.

"My favorite fucking flavor," I grunt before diving back in.

My tongue pushes into her opening, flicking up and down the walls of her pussy. I need more, so much fucking more. A growl leaves my mouth as I push against her mound and shift my attention to her clit. I flatten out my tongue while sucking on that hardened little bud.

"Fuck, Travis! Don't stop!" Lili's hands grip my head, pulling me closer. If I suffocate while eating out her pussy, I'll die a fucking happy man. Her thighs tighten around me, and her body seizes up as her orgasm takes over.

It's the most beautiful thing I've ever seen. Lili coming undone beneath me. *Because of me.*

I lick until her muscles relax, and only then do I move upwards. I reach for the string of foil wrappers and rip one open. Rolling the condom over my length before I line myself up with her entrance.

There's always something about the first moment I slide into her. A feeling of being home, being complete, overtakes me. "You complete me, Liliana Valentino." I whisper into her ear as I bottom out inside her.

I can't tell if the sigh she responds with is because of my words or from me filling her up. I'll take either.

I hook an arm underneath her knee as I push her leg up against her chest. Her right leg wraps around my waist, and I lose myself in the feeling of sliding in and out of her. Nothing feels as good as she does. I used to think scoring a goal was the best high I'd ever achieve.

I was wrong. Being inside Lili is next fucking level.

My thrusts increase in speed, as Lili's nails claw down my back and her hips lift to meet my rhythm. "I need you to come for me again, babe. I need to feel your pussy choke the shit out of my cock," I tell her.

"Oh god!" she cries out. "Travis."

Her pussy tightens around me, quivering with the impending explosion. I circle my hips and grind down on her clit with each thrust, hitting somewhere deep inside her. I can feel my own release building.

"Now, Lili. Come for me," I coax.

Lili's nails dig into my back. I wouldn't be surprised if she's drawn blood. "Shit. Fuck," she hisses as her entire body stiffens, and I follow her over the edge.

My thrusts become rigid as I fill the condom

inside her. "Fuck me," I huff out as I fall next to her on the mattress.

"I believe that's what you just did to me." Lili laughs.

Wrapping an arm around her body, I drag her closer to my side. "And I plan to do it again... after a brief, five-minute intermission."

Chapter Seventeen

Liliana

"Hey, Lili, your phone won't stop ringing, babe," Travis's voice calls out through the bathroom door.

"Can you bring it here?" I ask him while switching off the shower. I'm honestly surprised he didn't join me. There's a first time for everything, I guess.

Travis walks into the bathroom, my phone in his hand and a very pissed off expression on his face. "Why the fuck is Grayson Monroe calling you?" he asks between clenched teeth.

I smile as I tug my cell from his grip. It rings out before I can answer Gray's call. "He's a friend," I tell Travis.

"Friend, huh? What kind of friend?"

"Are you jealous?" I laugh. "You have no reason to be jealous, Travis. Gray's family is... friends with mine. I've known him practically my whole life. I'm also friends with his sister, but I'm guessing that won't bother you as much." My phone rings in my hand, Gray's name flashing up on my screen again. I swipe the green button to answer the call, but before I can bring the phone to my ear, Travis snatches it out of my hand. "What the fuck?" I yell out as I watch him disconnect the call.

"You're not talking to that fucker while you're naked, Lili," Travis grunts.

I look down at myself, then back up again. "It's a phone call. He can't see me." I roll my eyes as I grab a towel and wrap it around my body before plucking my phone out of Travis's hand, with every intention of calling Grayson back. My ringtone echoes through the bathroom before I have the chance. "Gray, why on earth are you blowing up my phone?" I answer, while keeping my eyes glued to Travis in defiance.

"I heard a disturbing rumor, Lil, and thought I'd come straight to the source," Gray says.

"Yeah? What rumor would that be?" I ask him. Given my last name, it could be any number of things. Only a few of them true.

"The one where people are saying that you're dating Travis O'Neil. Tell me you're not dating a hockey player, Lil."

"I am very much dating Travis." I grin into the phone. Then quickly pull the receiver back from my ear at the onslaught of curses coming from the other end of the line. "Okay, Gray, nice chat but I gotta go."

"Lil, be careful," he says. "I don't want to see you get hurt."

"I really like him, Grayson. And he's good to me." My gaze is still locked on Travis's.

"You can tell the fucker if he hurts you, I'll rip his heart out of his chest," Gray grunts.

"You'd have to take a number for that." I laugh.

"See you soon, Lil."

"How come you never mentioned this little

friendship with Monroe?" Travis asks as soon as Gray cuts the call.

"I have a lot of friends." I shrug. "Do you want a list?"

"If that list includes the family who owns the team I'm looking to get traded to, yes, I do."

"I..."

What am I supposed to say? That I purposely didn't tell Travis I knew the Monroes. That I didn't want him to ask me to *pull strings* to help get him signed with the Knights. Not that he's given me that impression. But, in my experience, everyone wants something from me eventually. And I just didn't want Travis to fall into that category. Not yet. I wanted to enjoy the blissful ignorance for a bit longer.

"Lili? What's wrong?" Travis inches closer to me, reaching out and pulling me into his arms.

"Not that I thought you were like that, but I didn't tell you because you mentioned how much you wanted to go to Vancouver and I..."

"You thought I'd ask you to call in a favor or something?" Travis tightens his grip on me.

"I didn't want to give you the *opportunity* to ask," I admit.

I feel the deep inhale of his breath, as his chest

rises and falls against my face. "Babe, look at me." Travis cups my cheeks, forcing me to meet his eyes. "I will never—and I mean *never*—ask you to do something like that for me," he says. "I love you, Lili. I love everything about you. I'm with you because I love you, not because of any fucking connections you might have."

"I love you too." I smile. "I'm sorry."

"You don't need to be sorry." Travis's lips land on mine in a featherlight kiss. Then he smiles against my mouth. "I love you," he repeats.

"I love you too."

"I wish you didn't have to go."

"Me too," I groan at the reminder. A whole month in Italy without Travis is going to be pure hell. Tears start to fall down my cheeks.

"I'm going to miss you, so damn much," he says.

"Not half as much as I'm going to miss you."

Travis wipes the tears from my cheeks. "Please don't cry. It breaks my heart, Lili."

"I'm sorry." I take in a huge breath. "Promise to call me every day."

"At least five times," he confirms.

My mom sits in the empty chair beside me. "I hate seeing you like this," she says.

"Like what?" I ask as I continue to stare out the window. The vastness of the night sky seems never-ending.

"Like you're miserable."

"I'm not miserable," I reply, finally turning my attention to her. "A month is just a really long time."

"I know it is." She nods. "You really like him, huh?"

"I love him." I keep my voice low. The last thing I need is for the rest of the family to hear me.

"I can tell," Mom says. "I'm sorry, Lil. I know it seems like a long time, but the month is going to fly by and you'll be back in New York before you know it."

"I doubt it's going to fly by, Mom," I mutter before looking out the window again.

"You could invite him to come for a weekend or something," she suggests.

My head snaps back around, and I raise my

brows at her like she's lost her mind. "I don't think Dad would be on board with that idea."

"I can handle your father." She smirks, and I shake my head.

"I think Travis has had enough threats to his life from my family."

"And yet he's still with you, which says a lot."

"It does. But dating me shouldn't come with so much baggage."

"Your father loves you, Lil. He doesn't know how to handle you being an adult."

I suck in another huge breath as I look my mother in the face. "Travis asked me to move to Vancouver with him."

I watch her eyes widen before they flick around the jet's interior, and she quickly lowers her voice to a whisper. "Vancouver, as in Canada?"

I nod.

"What do you want to do?"

"I want to be with him. If he gets traded, I'm going to go with him," I tell her.

"Okay." She sighs. "We're going to have to plan this right, and we might have to pull Nonna in to break the news to your father."

"For someone who's supposed to be next in line

to manage the empire, he sure is a big mama's boy." I laugh.

"They all are."

"Thanks, Mom. I love you," I say, while wrapping my arms around her.

"I love you more than anything in this world, Lil. If this is what you want, then I will find a way to make sure you get it."

I can see the tears forming in my mother's eyes. And I realize this probably hits a little too close to home for her. She lost both of her parents because their families, our families, didn't want them together. And something about the determination in her voice tells me she refuses to let history repeat itself.

Chapter Eighteen

I've been telling Lili that a month apart is nothing. That she'll be back in my arms before we know it. We're only halfway through that month and I'm desperate to see her. We call, Facetime, and text all day every day but it's not the same as having her here.

Fuck, my cock gets hard at just the thought of being able to touch her again.

The next two weeks cannot come fast enough. The time difference means I'm staying awake later, just so I don't miss her calls. The lack of sleep, the ache I feel in every fiber of my body from being apart from her is messing with me.

It's also messing with my game. Which is fucked. Nothing has ever affected how I played before. I didn't know falling in love would impact every aspect of my life.

Would I change it if I could? Stop myself from falling so hard, so fast? Fuck no.

"You look like shit," Logan says as he plops his ass down next to me on the bench. We're in the second period, playing against the Knights on our home turf. We have no fucking chance of winning this game, and knowing that fucking sucks.

"How about you focus more on staying upright on your blades and less on what I look like?" I counter.

"Fuck off," he says while shaking his head.

"O'Neil, you're up," Coach calls out from behind us, and I propel myself over the boards.

I purposely shove Monroe into the Perspex at full force, not slowing down a bit.

"Fucking asshole," he grunts at me as we fight for the puck.

It takes everything I have, but I'm finally able to speed off in the opposite direction with that little black disk in my possession. I break away, Logan on my right and two fucking Knights coming up behind us. Pass to Logan and speed up to get into position. I'm in front of the net when he slaps it back to me. I line up my shot and hit the puck through the small opening between the goalie's legs. I jump and pivot, my stick in the air as my line joins me in celebrating the goal. The whole arena roars along with us.

"Fuck yes!" I yell out.

"You got lucky. It won't happen again," Monroe says as I pass him.

"That's called skill, not luck."

A wicked smile crosses his face. "How's Liliana?"

My spine straightens. I know Lili says they're just family friends. But something about the way he asks that question turns my blood cold. "What the fuck did you just say?" I push up against his chest.

"I didn't stutter. How's Lil? We have a weekend off next week. I might head over to the estate in Italy and find out for myself," he says.

My stick drops to the ground, followed by my

gloves, before my right hand connects with his jaw so fucking quick his head snaps to the side. "Keep my girlfriend's name out of your fucking mouth," I hiss at him.

"Or what?" He shoves back at me.

"I don't care who you think you are, Monroe. I will fucking end you if you so much as think about her."

He laughs. "Good. Keep it that way, because if you fucking hurt her, I'm going to enjoy hunting your ass down," he says before skating back across the ice.

"What the fuck was that about?" Logan asks as I make my way over to the penalty box.

"Nothing." I close myself inside without having to be told. I knew it was coming.

That fucker didn't even retaliate. He didn't hit back. Why the fuck not?

"I miss you." Lili's voice fills my ears as her face lights up my laptop screen.

"Two more weeks, babe. Make sure you don't

have any plans, because I'm not letting you out of my bed," I tell her.

She smiles. "Sounds like heaven."

"It might not be heaven, but I'll definitely make you see stars." I smirk.

Lili chews on her bottom lip. "So... I had an interesting phone call earlier today..."

"Really? With who?"

"Gray," she says, and I roll my eyes. I hate the familiarity that she has with that asshole.

"What he want?"

"First, to brag that the Knights kicked your asses tonight. And then to tell me that you need to learn how to hit harder," she says.

"Hit harder, huh? I'll be sure to knock a few teeth loose next time." I laugh while shaking out my right hand. My knuckles are still bruised from the blow I landed on him.

"I watched the highlights. What'd he say to you to make you hit him?"

"Nothing," I grunt.

"Travis, what'd he say?" she pins me with a glare, and I groan.

"Lili, I get very limited time to talk to you. I'd rather not waste it on discussing some other guy. Now, how was your day?"

169

"Same, same. I ate, drank wine, and shopped. What else is there to do in Italy?"

"I wish I was there with you," I tell her.

"Me too. Two more weeks and I'm all yours." She smiles.

"Anything else happen?"

"Nothing at all. It's weird. Feels like something is going to happen, but no one is saying anything." She sighs. "I've been dropping hints about Canada by the way."

"We don't even know if I'm going yet, babe. We shouldn't be poking the beast with uncertainties," I tell her. It goes without saying that *the beast* is her father.

"You'll get it. You deserve it. I've never seen a better hockey player in my life." Lili smiles at me.

"You're biased, but thank you," I tell her.

"So... I was thinking... when the season's over, we should take a trip of our own."

"Yeah? Where do you want to go?"

"If it's with you, I'd go anywhere," she says.

"Name a place in the world you haven't been and always wanted to see," I tell her, "and I'll take you there, Lil. Our season is almost over. We're not going to the playoffs."

"Mmm, it's going to sound boring," she says.

"Nothing with you will ever be boring. Where do you want to go?"

"I was thinking of renting a house, upstate. In the suburbs. A normal, run-of-the-mill house. No frills. Just the two of us... doing everyday, mundane things. Like grocery shopping and cooking and all that," she says.

I smile. "That sounds awfully domesticated."

"It's stupid. Don't worry about it," she says while waving a dismissive hand at the screen.

"It's not stupid. I love the idea. Let's do it. I'm going to find a house, and as soon as I'm free, I'm taking you away," I tell her.

"Are you sure? We can do something else, anything really."

"I'm sure. Nothing sounds better to me than being domesticated with you, Lili." It's the fucking truth too.

"Okay." A huge grin brightens her face. Who would have thought such a simple thing could make her so fucking happy?

"There is one condition, though," I tell her.

"What's that?"

"I'm doing all the cooking."

"I can cook, Travis." She rolls her eyes.

"Mhmm, you can. But I can do it better." I laugh.

I watched her burn ramen before. I mean, how the fuck do you burn ramen?

"Fine, I don't like cooking anyway," Lili says.

"How long do you give it before your family comes looking for you?" I ask out of curiosity more than anything else.

"So there's this rule..." she says. "We're not supposed to travel alone. Anywhere."

"Ever?" I lift a questioning brow. "Besides, you're not alone. You'll be with me."

"We're supposed to always have a family member with us, but I have an idea."

"You really have never been anywhere without a family member with you?" I attempt to clarify. That sounds a little insane.

"It's for our own safety. But it'll be fine. They're going to just have to let me go. I'm not giving them a choice," she says.

I smile. "Why do I get the feeling you've never had a rebellious stage, Lili?"

"Because I haven't. I've always done what was expected of me... pretty much. The only time I've ever been in trouble has been because of someone else, one of my cousins or Alessandro."

I laugh. "I like that you're a good girl."

"I'm not always good," she hums.

"Yes, you are."

"Really? So last night when I slipped my hands into my panties with thoughts of you on my mind, I was being good?"

"Fuck yes, you were," I grind out as my own hand reaches for my cock.

"And if my hand slips beneath the sheets now...? If I push my fingers inside myself, is that being good too?"

"You're such a good fucking girl. Tell me how you feel, Lili." I stare at her on my screen. Her face is flushed, her eyes clouding over with lust.

"Wet, I'm so wet, Travis," she moans.

"Mmm, that's my good girl. I want to watch you come, Lili. Press your palm down on your clit while you thrust those fingers in and out of your pussy. Imagine that it's my hand, my fingers bringing you pleasure."

Lili closes her eyes. "I wish it were you. You're so much better at this than I am. Your fingers always feel better than my own."

"It'll be me before you know it, babe."

"Mmm, I want your cock to fill me up. I want to feel you stretching me. I want to feel the weight of your body on top of mine. I want your lips on me. I want your..." Her words die off as her head tips back.

"Fuck. I want you so bad," she hisses through clenched teeth, and I know her orgasm is close.

"Come for me, babe. Show me how much you want me," I urge her, and she does just that.

Lili's mouth falls open on a silent scream. My own orgasm follows hers, my cum spilling out all over my stomach. She slowly opens her eyes and stares back at me.

"As good as that was, it's not the real thing," she says.

"I know. Two more weeks," I remind her.

"Two more weeks," she repeats. "I love you."

"I love you too, babe. Sweet dreams, Lili. Think about me."

"All my dreams are about you, Travis," she says right before she ends our call.

Chapter Nineteen

My hand rises to knock on the door. I should have called. I shouldn't just be turning up. I told Travis I wasn't getting back until tomorrow. I wanted to surprise him, but now that I'm here, I don't know if that was the best idea.

I drop my hand. I don't knock. Instead, I take the key out of my pocket and let myself in. I know he's here. His car was in the garage. The apartment is quiet, so quiet. Then again, after spending a whole month with my entire family holed up in the same house together, *everything* seems quiet in comparison.

"Travis?" I call out while clicking the door closed behind me.

I hear footsteps. Actually, I hear running before he appears in front of me in nothing but a pair of workout shorts. His eyes wide and his breaths coming out in pants.

"Lili?" He rushes forward. His arms wrap around my waist and he picks me up and spins around. "Fuck me, never leave again," he whispers into my neck.

"I won't," I tell him, holding him just as tight as he's holding me. I knew I was going to miss him. I just wasn't prepared for how damn much.

"What are you doing here? I mean, thank fuck you're here. But I thought you weren't getting back until tomorrow?"

"I had this grand idea of surprising you."

"Well, consider me surprised," Travis says before

his lips fuse with mine. "I missed you so fucking much," he repeats between kisses.

"I missed you too."

Travis carries me through his apartment, his hands gripping my ass, before our bodies fall onto his bed. He pulls himself up and just stares at me. "I need a moment," he says. "I just want to look at you."

I smile. "You've seen me every day."

"It's not the same. Seeing you in person is so much fucking better." His eyes roam over every inch of my face like he's trying to memorize it in case I disappear. I won't. I missed him way too much to ever leave him behind again.

"I agree." My hands reach out and stroke up and down his bare chest, over his pecs, along the grooves of his abs. "Have you been working out more?" I ask him.

"A lot more. I've had excess energy to burn off." He smirks.

"Well, I hope you saved some of that energy for me."

"Every part of me is all yours, babe." Travis kneels on the floor by the edge of the bed. He grabs onto my ankles and drags my body forward until my ass is almost hanging off the mattress. "I've missed your taste," he says, kissing his way from my knee up to my inner thigh. "Always so fucking sweet." His lips are all over me and his tongue slides along the outside of my pussy, so fucking close to where I need him.

"Travis, please," I beg.

"Please what?" He peers up at me.

My brows draw down. Staring at him like this with his head between my legs is only turning me on more. And the fact that he's holding out on giving me what I really want—where I really need his tongue— is pissing me off. "You know what I want," I growl at him.

"I'm a lot of things, babe. A mind reader isn't one of them. You'll have to be more specific." He smirks while his lips pepper featherlight kisses on my inner thighs.

"I want you," I tell him.

"Which part of me?"

"I want your mouth on me, Travis."

"It is on you," he says as he makes a show of kissing me everywhere except for where I need him the most.

"I want your tongue on my pussy, Travis, now," I grind out between clenched teeth.

"Well, shit, babe, all you had to do was ask." He

chuckles before he finally slides his tongue up the center of my folds.

"Oh god," I cry out, and my fingers tighten around the blankets beneath me. I'm so worked up that that first stroke of his tongue is almost enough to send me soaring.

Travis's hands push on my legs, spreading them as wide as they will go. I'm completely open to him. For him. His mouth latches on to me, sucking at my clit, while his tongue flicks over that sensitive bundle of nerves. My legs shake with the need to close them. He doesn't let me move though, his fingers digging into my flesh with a bruising grip as he feasts on me.

"Fuck, Travis!" I scream his name as my entire body detonates, an orgasm blasting through me. I look down as Travis continues to slowly lick me as I return to earth. He's staring up at me, his eyes filled with desire and something else I can't quite pinpoint.

"Fuck, I love you," he says, kissing his way up my body, over my belly button. He takes his time lavishing each of my breasts with his mouth before his lips finally land on mine.

I open for him instantly, tasting myself on his tongue. My hands tangle in his hair, pulling him closer to me. I'm already so worked up again.

"I need you," I tell him.

"You have me, Lili," he says, pulling back and staring down at me.

I lift my hips, grinding myself against his bare cock. *When did he lose his shorts?* I don't know, but I sure as hell am glad he did.

"I need you inside me, Travis," I attempt to clarify.

Travis reaches out towards the bedside table. I know what he's doing. I stop his movements, peering up at him while I bite down on my lower lip.

"I... I don't want..."

How do I tell him I don't want him to use a condom? I want to feel him inside me. I want to feel all of him with nothing between us...

"What do you want, Liliana? I'm going to need to hear the words," he says.

"I want to feel you. I don't want anything between us, Travis," I admit aloud.

"You sure?" He's staring into my eyes, looking for any sign that I'm not one hundred percent certain that I want this.

"I'm sure. But only if you do. It's okay if you don't."

A cocky smirk tips up his mouth. "You think I haven't thought about fucking you bare? Haven't fantasized about it? Fuck yes, I want you. I want you any fucking way you'll let me have you, Lili."

I lift my hips off the bed, grinding against him again. "Fuck me, Travis."

"With pleasure," he says while lining up his cock and slowly sinking inside me. I watch as his eyes roll back in his head. "Fuck me, Lili," he groans, his jaw set tight. "This might be quicker than either of us wants it to be. It's been a while, and you feel fucking amazing." He drags his cock out before slamming it back in.

My legs wrap around his waist. I push at his chest and flip us over. I'm so desperate for him as my palms land on his pecs, supporting my weight as I lift my hips and slide down onto his cock over and over again.

His hands are all over me, setting my skin alight with pleasure as he explores every inch of my body with those fingers. Needing something more, I take one of his arms and position it between us.

Travis doesn't need directions. He instantly presses down on my clit, rubbing circles, and I continue to ride him as my pleasure builds. "Fuck, Lili, your pussy is choking the fuck out of me. I need you to come," he says. "Now." He grunts as his hips piston upward, his cock twitching inside me as he spills his release.

I collapse on top of his chest as my own release takes over me. I can feel my body trembling with the force of it.

"I love you, so fucking much." Travis says as his hands brush along my spine.

"I love you," I tell him. "Thank you."

His chest jostles with his laughter. "What are you thanking me for?"

"For being you."

Chapter Twenty

O f all the places in the world Lili could have asked me to take her, she chose a suburban home in upstate New York. She's told me that, as much as she loves and appreciates her family, she's envious of my *normal* upbringing.

I can't even pretend to imagine what her child-hood was like. Her family loves hard. That's not an issue, but the element of danger that comes with what they do can't be an easy thing to live with. The constant need to be on alert, never knowing what someone's motives are... I've noticed the way Lili assesses every room she enters.

The only time she ever appears truly relaxed is when she's with me, in my apartment, locked in our own little cocoon we've created. Which is why I can't fucking wait to get her out of the city for a whole week. Just the two of us.

"How'd your parents take the news?" I ask her, dropping an affectionate hand to her thigh. I flick my eyes in her direction. She's chewing on her bottom lip while looking across at me from the passenger seat of my car.

"I only told my mom, and she promised not to tell dad until after we left," she says, and I laugh.

"Really, what's he going to do, babe? Lock you in a dungeon?"

"I wouldn't put it past him." She shrugs. "But it's not that. He's just got a lot going on right now, and I don't want to add to his stress."

When Lili returned from Italy, she mentioned how her grandfather was retiring and her father was taking over. She was nervous as hell to bring it up. Like what her father does for a living has anything to do with whether or not I want to be with her. It doesn't. I couldn't care less if the man was the devil himself. I'd still want to be with his daughter. There is nothing that could make me not want her.

"I think his not knowing where you are is going to stress him out more than it would if he knew," I tell her.

"Please, he's going to know where I am within minutes of stopping to wonder why I'm not home." Lili rolls her eyes. "But my mom will make sure he doesn't come find us."

"Okay." I slide my hand up and take hold of her palm. "Are you ready to spend the next week in domesticated bliss with me?"

"I think I'm more excited about this trip than I was when I went to Disney as a kid," Lili says with a huge smile on her face.

"I beat Disney? Shit, babe, way to boost my ego."

"Your ego doesn't need boosting. But you are way better than Disney," she tells me. "Although this drive is going to take forever. We should have taken the jet."

"It's only three and a half hours. Besides, I like road-tripping with you."

"Three and a half hours is a long-ass time. We could have been there by now."

"Wanna play a game?" I suggest.

"Depends on what it is and if I'm likely to win."

One thing I've learned about Lili is her competitive nature is stronger than mine. Don't get me wrong... I fucking love to win. But Lili? She *has* to win. I'm assuming it has something to do with her parents letting her beat them at whatever she was playing as a child. My parents never *let* me win anything. If I won, it was because I was the better player.

"This isn't the kind of game you win or lose, babe. It's just... creative."

"Okay, what's the game?"

"What's their story? My parents used to play it with me when we went on road trips together."

"Explain it to me."

"You look around at other cars and make up the story for the people inside," I tell her. "Like there, that Beamer. Middle-aged guy. He's on his way back from a boring day at a job he hates. He's going home to an empty house. He chose a career over love and lives a sad, lonely life."

"That's horrible!" Lili gasps.

"It happens. It's life. What do you think his story is?" I ask her.

"Mmm, let's see." She appears to consider her options for a minute. "I've got it. He's a hitman, disguising himself as the average Joe, because that's how they go undetected. He has the body of his target currently wrapped in plastic in the trunk of his car and he's on his way to dispose of it. But not before he sends proof of his kill to whomever hired him. Then he'll burn the Beamer in the woods somewhere and find his way back home to his loving wife and kids, who all have no idea what he really does for a living."

I look over at my girlfriend, my eyes wide and my jaw slightly dropped. "You and I had very different upbringings, Lili."

"What? My story was way more creative than yours. I win." She smirks while crossing her arms over her chest.

"If there was a winner, you'd be it, babe. But there's not. So, no, you don't win."

"What's the point of playing a game if you can't win?"

"For fun?"

"Travis, you're a professional athlete. You're literally paid millions of dollars to *win*."

"Which is why I can play a game with my girl-friend without the need to win." I shrug. "Besides, I won the fucking lottery of a lifetime the day I met you. I don't think anything else can ever compare to that."

"What about when you win the Stanley Cup?" She lifts a challenging brow in my direction. I like that she says *when* and not *if*. Her belief in me is unwavering. Lili is my biggest cheerleader, besides my mom.

"Well, *when* that happens, I imagine it still won't compare to winning you," I tell her.

"You're a horrible liar, Travis." Lili laughs.

"Okay, it'll compare, but I'd still pick you over the Cup."

An hour into the trip, Lili closed her eyes and finally fell asleep. A few more hours after that, I was killing the engine and jumping out of the car.

I slowly click the door shut, walk around to her side, open her door, unplug her belt, and scoop her up into my arms.

"What are you doing? Where are we?" Lili asks.

"We're here, babe," I tell her, kicking the car door shut and walking us towards the house.

Her head pops up, and her arms wrap around my neck as she looks around. "We're here? Put me down. I can walk."

"But I like carrying you." Shifting her weight to one arm, I approach the keypad, type in the code I was given, and push the front door open.

"Wait," Lili says before I can step foot inside.

"What?"

"I just want to tell you that I love this place and thank you."

I lean in and kiss her. "You haven't even seen it yet, babe."

"I don't need to. I already love it," she says.

I set Lili on her feet once we're inside the small entryway. It's a quaint little cottage, advertised as a two-bedroom, two-bath house that backs onto a lake. Definitely not the kind of luxury Lili is accustomed to.

"It's perfect, Travis," she hums, spinning around while taking in the open living area. I follow her as she walks through to the kitchen and then continues down a little hallway to the bedrooms; she peeks inside both before heading back out again. "This is going to be the best week ever."

"It is," I agree, while wrapping my arms around her. I place a kiss on her forehead. "Let me go and get the bags from the car and then we can figure out what we want to do for dinner."

"I can help," she says.

"Nope, I got it. Sit your pretty ass down," I tell her, slapping her ass before I walk back towards the door.

I grab our bags, slam the trunk shut, and turn around. The feeling I'm being watched has me scanning the street before a black sedan pulls away from the curb. I try to shake off my paranoia and slip inside the house, making sure to lock the door behind me just in case.

"You sure your father didn't have you followed?" I call out to Lili.

She gets up from the sofa and turns to me. "I don't think so. Why?"

"No reason." I shrug.

"You wouldn't have asked me that for no reason," she says, walking past me to the front door. She peers out the small pane of glass on the side.

"I just had that feeling like I was being watched. It's nothing."

"Did you see anyone?"

"No, just a car that was parked two houses down. It drove off, though. I'm sure if it was your father's men, they wouldn't just drive off. They'd probably park their asses in the driveway."

"They would," she says.

"So what do you feel like having for dinner?" I ask while attempting to change the subject.

"Mmm, we're going to have to get some supplies. But tonight, let's go find a diner or something," Lili suggests. "I'm just gonna check in with my mom first. I told her I'd call when we got here."

"Okay, I'll take these to the bedroom." I gesture to the bags before carrying them down the hall.

Chapter Twenty-One

I hole up in the corner of the room and dial my father's number. I didn't want to freak Travis out, but I need to make sure I'm not being followed. And if I am, that it's because my father sent some of his men. In our world, there is no such thing as a coincidence, and I'm not stupid enough to ignore obvious warning signs. Even if they turn out to be nothing. I'd rather play on the side of caution.

"Liliana, you okay?" Dad asks.

"I'm okay," I tell him.

"How's Cooperstown?"

"Did you have me followed?"

"No. Your mother only just informed me about your little road trip."

"Oh." Shit, I really was hoping those were his men parked out on the street.

"Liliana, what's going on?"

"It's probably nothing." I sigh as I start peering out the closest window.

"Tell me anyway."

"Travis went to get our bags out of the trunk. He said there was a car in the street that drove off when he saw it. He thought it might have been some of your men."

There's a silence on the other end of the line for a moment.

"I'm coming to get you," Dad says.

"No. Don't do that. Please, Dad. Like I said, it's probably nothing," I tell him.

"I'm not taking the chance."

"Dad, please don't. I need this. Please, just... I really want to spend the week here."

My father lets out a string of expletives in rapid Italian. Things he always told me to never repeat as a kid. "I'm sending your brother and Zio Luca."

I groan. Maybe I shouldn't have called him. "I'm fine, honestly."

"They'll just scope out the town, Liliana. I'll tell them to stay out of sight. You won't even know they're there."

"Doubtful," I huff.

"I love you," Dad says. "Are you carrying?"

"I am." I don't always strap up, but that's because there's usually a gun within reach wherever I am. So I packed two, one in my purse and one in my luggage.

"Good. Make sure to keep it close. And remember: shoot first, ask questions later," he says.

"Thanks, Dad."

"Your uncle and brother will be there within the hour."

I look up and down the street as Travis and I walk

into the little diner we found. "You okay?" he asks me.

"Uh-huh, fine," I say, spotting a black sedan like the one he mentioned a block down from us. It's too far away to see who's inside it, though. My hand tightens on my purse as I let Travis lead me through the door.

"You seem really on edge, babe. What's going on?"

"I'm sorry. I just... I'm not used to being alone," I tell him.

"You're not alone. I'm here." He waits for me to slide into the booth before lowering himself down opposite me.

"I know that. Sorry. It's just going to take a second to get used to." I smile at him.

"Take all the time you need," he says.

I pick up the menu and start reading the contents. "What do you feel like having?"

"What I want isn't on this menu." Travis smirks, and I feel the blush rise up my chest.

"How about we save that for dessert? Back at the cottage..."

"Or I could lay you across this table, spread your thighs apart, and have your body writhing within seconds of my tongue worshiping that pussy of ours."

"*Ours?* When did my body parts become ours?" I laugh while my thighs squeeze together, trying to ease some of the ache the picture he's painted is causing.

"Since you became mine."

The waitress comes over to the table, interrupting Travis's dirty talk. And we both order burgers, fries, and a couple of Cokes.

"So, I got a call from my agent today," he says.

"What'd he say?"

"I got an offer, a really good one."

"From?"

"Vancouver."

My eyes widen and my lips split into a grin. I really am so proud of him. "Travis, that's fantastic. Why didn't you tell me sooner? This is what you've been waiting for."

"I haven't accepted it yet." He shrugs.

"Why the hell not?"

"Because I wanted to talk to you about it first. This doesn't just affect me, Lili. I'm not going without you. So if you tell me you can't leave New York, then that's where I'll be staying."

"Travis, Vancouver is your dream. You are not giving up your dream for me."

"You are my new dream," he says.

"We're going to Vancouver. Call your agent, right now, and tell him you're accepting that offer." I cross my arms over my chest. "Or I'm calling Mr. Monroe and telling him myself."

"Are you sure? You're really going to come with me?"

I can hear the hope in his voice. I nod. "Yes."

Travis leans over the table. His hand wraps around the back of my neck as he pulls me closer before his lips slam down on mine. "I fucking love you."

"I love you too," I say as excitement over what the future holds for us runs through me.

By the time we return to the cottage, I'm more relaxed. It might have had something to do with the text message I got from Alessandro. He snapped a picture of Travis and me at the diner and sent it through. I honestly thought that coming away without any of my family being around would be easier. I didn't expect the anxiety it would create. I haven't told Travis that I called my dad. And I didn't tell him that my brother and uncle are now in town. I'm hoping that they follow my father's orders and stay out of sight.

"You wanna jump in the hot tub?" Travis asks me.

I look past him, at the sliding glass doors. There's a hot tub on the deck that overlooks the yard and the lake at the edge of the property. My nose scrunches up. "How many people do you think have fucked in that thing?"

"Probably a lot. We can add to that number." Travis waggles his eyebrows up and down.

"Yeah, let's not." I shake my head. "That's disgusting and a UTI waiting to happen."

"You wanna watch a movie?"

"Sure, but I'm picking it." I plop down on the sofa, pull the throw blanket from the top, and cover myself.

"I wouldn't have it any other way," Travis says, sitting down next to me. He picks me up and places my back against his chest, his legs on each side of my body.

"You know, a girl could get used to this." I sigh.

"Get used to what?"

"Domesticated bliss with *the* Travis O'Neil."

"I hope so, because I don't plan on letting you go."

I flick through the channels, settling on a rerun of *50 First Dates*. Halfway through the movie, I look up at Travis. "What would you do if I forgot us?"

"I wouldn't ever let you forget, Lili. Besides, how the fuck could you forget that you love this face?" He draws a circle in the air for good measure.

"It is a really pretty face," I tell him.

"Did you just call me *pretty*?" Travis laughs.

"You and I both know how good looking you are. Don't pretend you don't know that face of yours is breaking hearts all across the country."

"As long as it's not breaking yours. I don't give a shit about anyone else."

My phone vibrates on the coffee table. I reach out, pick it up, and find another message from Alessandro. "It's my brother," I tell Travis before tapping on the notification.

ALESSANDRO:

They were paps. We've sent them on their way.

ME:

Thank you.

ALESSANDRO:

Anytime, sis. Have fun, but not too much fun. I'm heading back to the city.

ME:

Dad's letting you leave me here alone?

ALESSANDRO:

Don't be ridiculous. Zio Luca is staying in town.

I roll my eyes. *Of course he is.*

ME:

I love you.

ALESSANDRO:

Love you.

I set my phone back down on the table and catch Travis's eye. "Everything okay?" he asks.

"Uh-huh, perfect." I roll over, crawl my way up his body, and close my mouth over his.

Chapter Twenty-Two

This has been the best break I've ever had. And it one hundred percent has to do with the company. Spending an entire week alone with Lili has cemented the fact that I do not want to live without her. I want her in my bed every fucking night. I want to start every day with her.

Which is why, now that I'm driving her back into the city, every fiber of my being wants to turn around and go back. I know as soon as we hit the city limits again, the reality will kick in. She'll want to go home to her parents' house and she has to return to work in the morning.

"You're awfully quiet," Lili says, looking at me from the passenger seat.

"Mhmm."

"What's wrong?"

"I don't want to give you back. I want to keep you to myself and not have to share you with everyone else," I tell her.

"You're not sharing me with anyone, Travis. I'm yours."

"I have to share you with your family." I know I sound ridiculous. I can hear how unreasonable it is the moment the words leave my mouth. None of that changes the fact that I mean it.

"It's only another six weeks, and we're both going to be in Vancouver. Together," she says.

We decided that I'd settle in first, and Lili is planning on coming up when the season starts. I didn't like the idea. I wanted us to leave New York together, but she insists she needs to give her job more than a few weeks' notice.

"I'm also going to fly out and see you every weekend," she adds.

"I know, but I don't want to spend one day apart, babe."

"I'm sorry..." Her voice dips and her eyes drop to her lap.

"It's not your fault." I pick up her hand and bring it to my mouth. "I had a really great week."

"Me too." She smiles, and I swear I will do anything and everything in my power to see that smile on her face as often as I can.

"So, when are we telling your parents you're moving?"

"We're not. *I am*. After you leave town. It'll be safer that way." She laughs.

"I'm not scared of your father, Lili," I tell her. It's a lie. I'd be stupid not to be a little afraid of the man, but I'm not ever going to admit that out loud or show that fear to anyone. She needs to know I'm here for her. That there's nothing her family can do to run me off.

"You'd be the first," she says. "He'll be fine. Besides, he has Josie to focus on now." Lili beams. "I always wanted a sister, and now that I have one, all that attention can go to her."

While we were away, Lili found out her parents adopted her cousin's girlfriend. She mentioned something about Josie being in the foster care system and not in a good place. Her mother and father wanted to help the girl, so they adopted her. I was shocked. Adopting a teenager is a lot, but they seemed to not even second-guess the real commitment of taking on another kid.

"You're not jealous that you're not the only princess of the palace anymore?" I grin.

"First, I'm not a princess and I don't live in a palace." Lili narrows her glare at me. "Second, I've been spoiled my entire life. Josie deserves to have a turn."

"I've been to your family home. It's a fucking palace, babe, and you are most certainly a princess," I tell her. "Do you want to come back to my place?"

"I do, but I should go home first. I'll come over later, though... if you want."

"I always want you there," I tell her. I pull up to the Valentino estate a few minutes later and turn in my seat. "I can't fucking wait to start our lives in Canada."

"Me too." Lili leans over the center console and

presses her lips to mine. "I'll see you soon, hotshot," she says before climbing out of my car.

When I walk into my apartment, I find my mother in the kitchen. "Mom, I didn't know you were coming today." I close the distance and kiss her cheek before stepping back and looking at all the groceries lined up on the counter.

"I knew you'd be back today. You needed food, Travis."

"You do know I can feed myself," I tell her.

"No, you can't," she huffs while shaking her head in my direction.

"Are you planning on flying out to Vancouver every week to stock my fridge too?" I laugh, swipe up some bell peppers and carrots, and set them in the cold storage drawer.

"If I have to, I will. But you'll have Lili there. I have no doubt she'll make sure you eat."

"I have Lili here too."

"I know, but you also have me."

My mother cried when I told her I was moving to

Vancouver. She was happy for me, of course. Proud too. But knowing I would be so far away hit hard.

"It's not going to be forever," I remind her.

"I know that. But don't you dare have kids over there. My grandbabies have to live in New York, Travis. I won't have them in a different country."

"I'm not planning on giving you any grandkids for at least another twenty years, Mom." I smirk. Truth is Lili and I haven't even broached the subject of having kids. Not seriously. I honestly don't care either way. Though I can't help but wonder how she feels about it.

Would she want kids with me?

Once all the groceries are put away, Mom makes us each a cup of coffee. I lead her out to the balcony and sit down. "I'm going to miss this city," I tell her.

"This city is going to miss you. How was your little getaway?"

"Pure fucking bliss." I can feel myself grinning. It's just what happens whenever I think about Lili.

"Language," Mom scolds. "I'm glad you had a good time. We really like this girl, Travis."

"I really like her too."

"Good. Now, don't fuck it up."

"Don't plan on it." I'm never going to let Lili go.

It doesn't matter what life throws at us. I will never give up on this relationship.

"What about this one?" I point at a large three-story house on the screen in front of us. Lili and I have been sitting in bed scrolling through Vancouver real estate for the past hour.

"Why on earth do we need a house that big?" she asks me.

"Because you, my dear, are a princess who grew up in a palace, remember? I can hardly make you move to another country, only to have you live in a shack."

Lili glances at the listing again, her gaze focused on the address. "That's just down the street from Gray, same development and everything."

I press the red button on the tab, deleting the page. "That's in the *no* pile then."

"You do know you're going to have to play nice with him, right? He's going to be your captain."

"Yup, but I don't need to be neighbors with the guy."

"I wouldn't mind being neighbors with Kathryn. I'd be able to see Graycee all the time." Lili shrugs.

Kathryn is Grayson's girlfriend, and Graycee is their daughter. The girls were best friends in college until Kathryn went missing. She was gone for six years and just turned back up in Vancouver about a month ago.

"I don't have an issue with Kathryn and Graycee. They can visit as often as you'd like... if they leave Gray behind."

There isn't any real reason why I don't like the guy. His arrogance just rubs me the wrong way. I also don't like how *friendly* he is with my girlfriend.

"Look, we can live wherever you want, but I would like to be close to Kathryn and Gray. They're the only people I know in the area... It's not that I need friends, or family even, but it's going to take some time for me to get used to not being surrounded by people all the time. And you'll be away a lot during the season."

And now I feel like shit...

"If you like that development, we'll find a house there. All I want is you. I don't care where we live, babe. As long as you're there, it'll feel like home."

"I'm going to get my Zia Savvy to come and decorate. She's the best interior designer I know, and

I've always wanted her to do my house when I got my own. Is that okay?"

"Babe, it'll be your house, your home. You do not need to ask permission for anything," I tell her.

"It's *our* house, and I'm not asking permission. I'm asking for your opinion," she says.

"My opinion is I like whatever you like. I want what you want." I lean across the bed and kiss her gently before pulling back again.

Chapter Twenty-Three

Present Day

I'm numb. I've never felt this kind of terror before. I've never known this kind of pain. "He's going to be okay, Lil," Alessandro says while squeezing me tight in his arms.

My brother came through, did what I asked of him without question. He helped sneak me out of the house undetected. And by the time we arrived at the hangar, the pilots were ready to take off and all of my cousins, with the exception of Lorenzo, were on the jet waiting for us.

"You don't know that," I cry into his chest. It's where I've been since takeoff. I haven't said a word to anyone else. Alessandro led me to the back of the jet and sat next to me. As far as brothers go, I really did luck out.

"Lil, he's Travis fucking O'Neil. He is going to be okay," he repeats. "That guy takes harder hits than a bullet every time he's out on that ice."

"I'm not ready to lose him, Alessandro. I only just got him. I don't want to lose him," I say through hiccups.

"You're not going to lose him." My brother continues to rub his hands up and down my back.

I want to believe him. I desperately want him to be right, but I'm not an idiot. I know that just because someone says something with conviction, it doesn't make it true. And even if Travis is okay, if he does survive this, he's never going to want anything to do with me again. It's my fault he was shot. It's my fault he's in surgery. And it's my fault if this ruins his career... If he can never play hockey again...

I check my phone for the millionth time. Gray is supposed to message me as soon as Travis is out of surgery. There's nothing yet. That can't be a good sign.

Alessandro shifts me slightly as he retrieves his own phone from his pocket. "It's Pops," he says.

"I'm surprised he took this long," I grumble.

"He didn't do this, Lil. I know you don't want to believe that right now, but he really wouldn't do this to you."

"I don't want to talk to him right now. I honestly don't know if he did this or not, but it's the only thing that makes sense. Travis doesn't have enemies, other than Dad."

"Pops, what's up?" Alessandro answers his phone with a carefree tone while holding me against his side. "Yeah, no can do... sorry."

I can hear my father's voice through the speaker when Alessandro pulls it away from his ear slightly. He's pissed.

Good. Let him be pissed. Because right now, so am I.

"She might be your daughter, but she's my sister.

And you always tell me to protect her at all costs. Remember? To support her. And that's what I'm doing. I'm choosing her because she needs me," Alessandro says.

No one ever tells my father *no*. Not even us. My brother is risking his future with the family business, facing the full brute of my father's temper... for me.

"You need to give her time," he says. "And me some fucking credit, Pops. I'm not going to let anything happen to her."

I close my eyes, only to open them again when Travis's face pops up behind my lids. Can this jet go any faster?

When we land in Vancouver, there are three SUVs waiting for us. Alessandro and my cousin Enzo climb into one with me. The rest of my cousins fill the other two; they're headed to a rental property while we go straight to the hospital.

My hands shake. I'm so cold, but I can't seem to get warm. I dig my phone out of my pocket again and call Gray's number. He should have contacted me by now. The fact that he hasn't only increases my worry.

"Lil, you land?" he asks after the second ring.

"I'm on my way to the hospital. Is he...?" I swallow down the rest of my words. I can't voice them.

"They just rolled him out of the operating room. They've induced a coma," Gray says, and I continue to sob into the phone. "Lil, he's a tough one. He'll pull through. He just needs a little time to heal."

"What if he doesn't?" I ask. "What am I supposed to do?"

"Let's not talk about *what ifs* and focus on the facts. He's out of surgery. He's fighting, and trust me when I say that guy is not going to give you up so easily."

"I'll see you soon." I choke down the rest of my tears and hang up. Then I take a deep breath and look over at my brother and cousin. "He's out of surgery and in an induced coma."

"Okay, that's good. He's out of surgery," Alessandro says. "And an induced coma is different from a regular coma. It means that the doctors can wake him up when they think he's ready."

"I know." I wipe at my cheeks. I need to pull myself together. I really hope everyone is right. I need him to be okay. I can't fathom a world without him in it. I can't think of Travis not being here.

I also can't get my head around why this is happening. My brother is adamant that it wasn't our father, but I just can't think of anyone else who would want to kill Travis. He's not from our world. He doesn't have enemies lurking in every corner. And the only threats he's faced came directly from my family.

Did my announcement that I was moving in with Travis push my father to his breaking point?

I knew he wouldn't like it. And I knew he would be over the top about letting me go. But, at the end of the day, I really thought he would be able to put my happiness above anything else. I thought he would let me have this. I was wrong. My whole life has been scripted. Controlled. He's used to dictating where I can go, who I can be friends with, and who I have to avoid...

Why would that be different now?

The SUV stops at the entrance to the hospital, and Alessandro grips my hand in his as we walk in a few seconds later. Everything is a blur as my brother leads me through the winding halls. He stops to speak to someone and then we're guided to a room.

The lights are too bright, the sounds of machines beeping deafening, and the smell...

Why do hospitals have to smell so bad?

I drop Alessandro's hand and step closer to the bed. Closer to Travis. People are talking but I don't know what they're saying. It's all background noise as I stare down at the love of my life lying lifeless in the bed. A bunch of tubes and wires attached to his body. And the room starts to close in on me.

I hear my brother yelling before my knees give out, and I start falling. Blackness creeps in as some-one's hands grab at me.

"Travis." I sit up with a jolt.

"Shit, Lil, slow down," Alessandro says, grabbing my arms.

"What happened?" I look around the room. Enzo and Gray are both staring at me with concern on their faces. "What happened? Where is he?" I ask again, while trying to push out of my brother's hold so I can stand.

"Liliana, you passed out. Travis is fine. He's right there. You need to sit down," Alessandro says.

"He's okay?" I whisper.

"He's fine. He's right there. I spoke with his doctors. He's going to be fine, Lil," my brother assures me.

"Promise?"

The moment he hesitates, I know my brother is talking out of his ass. If he believed it, he'd tell me as much. But I know he won't make me a promise he can't keep.

"Lil, I promise the doctors are confident that he's going to be okay." Alessandro chooses his words carefully.

The door bursts open, and Travis's parents rush into the room. I take one look at his mother and guilt consumes me. "I'm so sorry," I choke out, the tears streaming down my face all over again.

"Oh, sweetheart, this is not your fault," Frances says as she tugs me into her arms. She's comforting me when I should be the one comforting her. Her lips press to the center of my forehead. "He's going to be okay."

I nod my head, but I'm not sure I believe her either. Frances squeezes once more before releasing me, and I watch as she approaches the hospital bed, silent tears falling down her face when she looks at her son. I position myself at the bottom rail. Alessandro follows me. His hand closes around mine as I stand here and look at Travis. This is my fault. He's in this bed because of me, and I have no idea what I'm supposed to do now.

"When is he going to wake up?" I don't know who I'm asking, but I ask it anyway.

"The doctors are going to wake him up tomorrow. They want him to rest overnight," Mr. O'Neil says.

I nod my head. Tomorrow. He's going to wake up tomorrow.

When Alessandro's phone rings out, breaking the silence, he excuses himself from the room. Enzo follows him out, and Gray steps up to my side. His hand replaces my brother's as he gives my palm a comforting squeeze.

"He wouldn't like you holding my hand, you know."

"I know," Gray says. "But you were my friend long before you were his."

"You should go home to your daughter."

"I'm not leaving you, Lil. That's not what we do. You never left my side when I needed it. I won't leave yours either," he says.

He's talking about when Kathryn ran away. I knew she left. I was the one who helped her disappear in the first place. Even though she never told me why until recently.

I hated watching him mourn her. I hated watching his heart break over and over again, when I knew she wasn't really missing. That she chose to leave him. But she was my best friend, and for whatever reason, she was adamant that he couldn't know where she was. I kept her secret. All those years, I kept her secret and did my best to help Gray move on. Not that he ever really did. The fact that he doesn't hate me right now is a miracle. Because if the roles were reversed, I'm not sure I'd be as forgiving.

"I need to know who did this," I whisper to Gray.

"We're going to find out," he says. "I promise we will find the person who did this."

"And if it was my father?" I keep my voice low. The last thing I need is for Travis's parents to overhear me and realize this is my fault.

"It wasn't your family, Lil. Your father isn't going to start a war with us."

Gray's wrong, though, because I know my father would go to war with anyone when it comes to his kids. *His family.* And taking me away is the biggest threat there is.

Chapter Twenty-Four

Something wet drops on my hand, my fingers. I blink my eyes open, and a bright light has me slamming them shut before slowly opening them again. I look down at my arm, wondering what's dripping.

"Lili?" My throat is sore, my voice hoarse.

Her head snaps up, and her tear-filled eyes land on mine. "You're awake. Shit. I need to get a doctor," she says, reaching over and quickly pressing a button above my head.

I lift my hand to her face and wipe the wetness from her cheeks. "What's wrong?"

"Travis, you were shot yesterday. How do you feel? That's a stupid question." She looks away and shakes her head.

"Why are you crying?"

"You were shot," she repeats.

I try to sit up, only to stop when a sharp, piercing pain rips through my abdomen. "Fuck." I grit my teeth.

"Don't move. Your parents are here. They just went to grab a coffee," Lili says. "Travis, I'm... I'm so sorry. I didn't know..."

"What? Why are you apologizing, babe?" I'm still trying to wrap my head around what's going on. But my brain feels foggy. I can only imagine how many drugs are running through my system.

"This is my fault," she whispers.

"Lili, babe, as much as my world starts and ends with you, my getting shot is not your fault." I reach out and take her hand.

Lili shakes her head. "I'm sorry. I should have

222

stayed away from you. If I had, this wouldn't have happened."

"I don't know what you're talking about, Lili," I tell her honestly, glance around the room, and look back at her again.

I was shot... I remember leaving practice yesterday. I remember the pain, the blood, the red lights. Envisioning her red lips...

"I love you. So damn much. I'm so sorry," Lili says.

Before I can respond, the door opens and my parents walk in. Followed by someone else. A doctor, if the lab coat and scrubs are anything to go by. Lili slips her hand free and steps away from the bed.

"Babe, it's okay. I'm okay," I tell her while trying to force myself up again.

"I... I'm sorry," she repeats with a fresh wave of tears streaming down her face.

"It's not your fault."

She offers me a sad smile before turning and running out of the room.

"Shit," I hiss out as I attempt to push up from the bed.

"Stop. You can't get up." My mom rushes to my side and gently presses down on my chest.

"I need to get her," I say.

"She'll be back. Just stay put," Mom tells me.

"I'll go talk to her." My dad nods in my direction before pushing through the door.

The doctor picks up my chart, glances down, then looks up at me. "Mr. O'Neil, you're one lucky man."

Lucky? My fucking girlfriend just ran out of the room in tears, and I'm stuck here, in this bed, unable to go after her. I don't consider that fucking lucky.

I keep that thought to myself, though.

"The projectile missed all major organs and we were able to control the bleeding. Barring infection, you should be able to make a full recovery in no time," he says.

"When can I get back out on the ice?" I ask. It's not my first concern right now, but it is a concern.

"That'll depend on your body and how it heals. The police are waiting to talk to you," he says, without giving me much of an answer.

"They can wait," my mother is quick to chime in.

"Mom, I need to speak to Grayson. Can you find my phone?" I ask her.

"Oh, he's just out in the hall. I'll send him in and go find your father and Liliana." She bends down and kisses my forehead. "Do not scare me like this ever again, Travis," she scolds, like I got myself shot on purpose.

"I won't," I tell her anyway.

The doctor follows my mother out of the room, and I'm left alone for a whole minute before Grayson walks in.

"Is Lili out there?" I ask him.

"She's with her brother," he says, and some of my panic eases with the knowledge that she's with her family.

"We need to talk." My eyes bounce between my teammate and the door.

"Hold that thought." Grayson raises a finger to his lips, urging me to be quiet. Then he sticks his head out the door and someone else walks in. It's Enzo, one of Lili's cousins. He pulls a black box out of his pocket and flicks a switch.

"What's that?" I ask. I really don't want to have this conversation in front of a Valentino.

"A scrambler," Enzo says. "Can never be too careful. Thin walls and all." He shrugs.

I nod and pretend to clear my throat. "Can you get me some water?"

"Do I look like your fucking nurse?" Enzo grunts.

"Please," I add, looking from him to Gray.

"You could just lay it out straight and say you

don't want me in here." Enzo sets the device on a nearby table, pivots on his heel, and stalks out of the room.

"What's going on?" Gray asks as soon as the door closes again.

"Whoever shot me... they said it was for Liliana right before they pulled the trigger," I tell him. "I need you to get me out of here, Grayson. If someone is after her, I can't be fucking stuck in this bed."

"If someone is after her, they'll have to get through her family first. And that's not going to happen. You get a good look at the fucker's face? The cameras were cut."

I shake my head. It's all a bit fuzzy still. "I don't remember." My eyes flick around the room. "I need to get out of here," I say, while pulling a bunch of wires from my chest.

"You just got shot, man. You should leave your ass in that bed."

"I need to get Lili," I tell him.

"She's with Alessandro. He's taken her back to the house."

"What house?" I stop what I'm doing and peer up at Grayson.

"A rental, near my place."

"Is it secure? I need to make sure she's okay."

"Why aren't you telling her family? They can protect her better than anyone else." He lifts a questioning brow.

"I don't want her knowing. I need you to find a way to make sure she's got security on her without anyone knowing why," I tell him, then add, "I know you have the resources to do that."

"I'll take care of it." Gray swipes up the little black box and walks out just as my mom and dad are walking in.

"You need to be resting, Travis." My mom lays a gentle hand on my arm.

"What I need is my girlfriend," I tell her.

"She's scared and processing. I have no doubt that she will be back," Mom says.

"Travis, lay your ass down before you do more damage. You need to heal. If you want to be any good for that girl, then you have to focus on healing properly," my father barks.

"I need her," I repeat, my voice quiet.

"I know, sweetheart. You just have to be a little patient with her, a little more understanding." Mom kisses my forehead.

I don't like this. I feel so out of control and fucking helpless. I know Lili blames herself, but if anything, she's the reason I'm still fucking here. It was her face that kept me awake until the ambulance arrived. It was her voice that kept me from giving into the darkness that threatened to take over. I had to get back to her. I couldn't leave her.

"Did you find my phone?" I ask my mom.

"I did." She opens a drawer next to my bed, pulls out my cell, and hands it to me.

I tap on my messages. I want to call Lili, but I don't think she's going to answer. She will read my words, though, so I settle for sending her a text.

ME:

> I love you. I know you're scared, and I'm sorry I caused you to feel that way. I need you to come back, Lili. Do not run from this.

ME:

> Please.

The notification pops up, telling me that she's read the message, but she doesn't reply.

Chapter Twenty-Five

I never really understood heartbreak. I didn't know it would feel like this. As if whoever I was before is gone. It's like my heart is shattering inside my chest and there isn't enough duct tape in the world to put it back together.

I also never expected to be the cause of my own

heartbreak. I did this to myself. I let myself believe that I could keep him. That I finally found a man who was worthy of me and I was going to get my happily ever after.

Except girls like me don't get that fairy tale. In my story, one heart has to break to ensure the other keeps beating. I will endure the pain, the despair. I'll endure it all if it means that Travis is okay. I won't be the reason he's no longer living. I refuse to be his downfall. Instead, I'll be my own. I'm giving myself another day to wallow in my grief before I'm going to bury all of these feelings somewhere deep down and carry on living a life that I no longer want.

I don't want to return to New York and pretend that I haven't left the other half of my soul behind. I don't want to carry on as if he never existed, but I don't have any other choice.

"Okay, we're doing this."

I peek my eyes open at the sound of Gray's voice and watch as he walks over to the window and spreads the curtains open.

"Go away." I roll over on the bed and bury myself under the covers.

"Nope, no can do. If you're going to have a pity party, then who better to join you than me, Lil? I am the master of self-loathing after all." Gray yanks at the blanket, pulling it off the bed completely.

"I don't want to talk about it," I tell him.

"Good, because neither do I. What I want to do is get drunk." He places two glasses down on the nightstand before shoving me over to make room for himself on the bed. "Why are you hiding out in here anyway?"

"I'm really not in the mood, Gray," I grumble.

"Too fucking bad. Sit your ass up and have a drink with me. You owe me that much," he says, laying the guilt trip on thick this time.

"I don't owe you shit," I groan.

"You helped my girlfriend disappear for six years, then sat by my side while I mourned her death, Liliana. You owe me."

"I helped *my best friend* disappear. I did it for her, and I'd do it again if I had to," I warn him.

"I just came from the hospital. Your boyfriend's all up in arms about checking himself out against medical advice to come and get you."

"He can't do that." I sit up straighter.

"It's not wise, but he can do it. If he wants. And he's determined to talk to you." Gray pours two glasses of whiskey and hands one to me.

"I'm going home. I can't be here," I tell him.

"Travis know that?"

"I can't be with him. It's because of me he almost got killed." I take the glass from Gray's hand, down the contents, and regret it instantly. My throat and chest burn from the liquor.

"Bullshit. That bullet had nothing to do with you, Lil," Gray says.

My brows furrow. "You don't know that."

"I do know that. If anything, it was probably because of us. Valentinos have no business in Vancouver, Lil."

"Travis took a bullet because of your family?" I punch his shoulder.

"Ow, damn it. Don't hit me."

"My boyfriend took a bullet that had your name on it, didn't he?" I hold out my glass, waiting for Gray to refill it.

"He did. So, you see, it had absolutely nothing to do with you." Gray smiles like he just solved world hunger or something.

"It doesn't matter. It would have happened because of me eventually. The world I live in, the kind we both grew up in, Gray... it's not meant for normal. And Travis is as normal as they get." I shake my head and stare into my whiskey. "I never should have got involved with him."

"So, what? You're going to stick to dating made men?" Gray raises his brows at me.

"I'm never dating again." I chug the rest of the amber liquid and set my glass down on the nightstand.

"Yeah, okay." He rolls his eyes. "You're being dramatic, Lil, and the only person you're hurting is yourself. Well, yourself and Travis."

"I'm not hurting Travis. I'm protecting him."

"What the fuck are you doing in here? Get off that fucking bed before I leave your ass to bleed all over it."

Gray and I turn towards the door at the sound of my brother's voice.

"Calm down. We're just talking," Gray grunts.

"You can talk without being on her fucking bed," Alessandro counters while storming into the room.

Gray pushes up from the bed and lands me with a glare. "Lil, call him," he says before barging past Alessandro and out of the room.

I look to my brother. "That was unnecessary, you know."

"Actually, it was very necessary. Pops is here."

My eyes widen. "What is he doing here?"

"What do you think? Looking for you."

"Tell him I don't want to see him." I reach down

and pick up the blankets Gray tossed on the floor. Then I lean against the headboard and bring my knees up to my chest.

"You can't avoid him forever, Lil, but if you really want, I can try to get you out of here before he figures out which room you're in."

I peer over at the door. I'm about to tell my brother to get me out of the house when my father's body fills the opening. "Alessandro, get out," he says, stepping into the room.

Alessandro looks at me. "You want me to stay?"

"I said get the fuck out," Dad yells, his jaw tense and his eyes narrowed at my brother.

Alessandro turns around, his arms folded over his chest. "And I'm asking my sister if she wants me to stay or not. If she says yes, then you'll have to drag my dead body out."

The corner of Dad's lips tip up, and there's a hint of pride in his eyes. He doesn't say anything, just raises a single brow and shoves his hands into his pockets like he's amused.

"Lil?" Alessandro looks over his shoulder at me.

"It's fine. Go," I tell my brother.

He nods once. "I'll be downstairs if you need me."

Dad waits for Alessandro to leave the room

before he closes the door and walks over to the bed. He sits on the edge of the mattress, right next to me. He doesn't say anything, but he doesn't have to. I know I hurt him. I know that my outburst before I left home hurt him a lot. I'm still not one hundred percent convinced he didn't do this, though, and I hate that I'm doubting my own father.

"I'm sorry," I whisper.

"For what?" he asks.

"I..." My words die off. I take a deep breath as a fresh bout of tears fall down my cheeks.

"Fuck. Liliana." Dad reaches out and pulls me into his chest as his arms wrap around my back. "Please don't cry," he says as he kisses the top of my head.

"It hurts," I sob. My fingers wrap around the lapels of his jacket.

"I know, sweetheart. He's going to be fine, though. I spoke with his doctor," Dad tells me.

I shake my head. "I can't..."

"It's okay. Just breathe." Dad rubs his hands up and down my back.

"He's... Seeing him in the hospital, all the tubes, everything... It was... I can't see that again."

"He's okay, Liliana," Dad repeats. "You want me to take you back to the hospital to see him?"

I shake my head again. "I can't. I have to stay away."

"Why?"

"Because I don't want to get him hurt more than he already is. I don't want our world to touch him."

"This wasn't your fault, Liliana. This had nothing to do with us," Dad tells me.

"We don't know that. *I* don't know that." I pull back and look up at him.

Dad sighs and runs a hand down his face. "It's not like I haven't wanted to fill his body with lead." He smirks. "But I would never do anything to hurt you, Liliana. Watching you fall apart like this is fucking destroying my soul."

I can see the truth in his eyes. I believe him. I don't know if that just makes me naïve or desperate, though. Because I also *want* to believe him. "I'm sorry."

"Why don't you just talk to him?"

"I can't."

"Tell me something... What made you want to move to fucking Canada of all places with this guy?"

"I love him, Daddy." I lift one shoulder in a half shrug.

"Why?" he asks me.

"Because he's... he's everything. Kind, patient,

and when he looks at me, I feel like I'm the center of his world. When I'm with him, I feel a peace I've never known before. And when I'm not, all I do is count down the time until I see him again." I wipe at my cheeks. "You always showed me what love looks like, the way you love Mom, the way you treat her. That's the kind of love I've always wanted to find myself. And I did find it. Travis is that kind of love for me."

"Then why are you so ready to walk away from it?"

"Because I love him too much to watch him get hurt again," I admit.

"Liliana, there are no guarantees in life. No matter what you do for a living or how you live. If you want me to take you home, I will. If you want me to take you to the hospital to see him, I will. But you shouldn't let fear dictate your decisions."

"I want to go home."

"Okay." Dad tugs me back against his chest. "I need to do a few things first. We'll leave in the morning," he says.

I nod my head against him and tighten my arms around his waist. "Thank you."

"I love you, Liliana."

"Don't be too hard on Alessandro. I made him

promise not to tell you where we were," I say. "And you taught us never to break our promises."

"Your brother makes his own choices. And he chose you. That's not something I'll ever be mad at either of you for. You should always choose each other." My father squeezes me one more time, then pushes up from the bed and makes his way to the door.

"Dad, I love you too," I call after him.

He nods before walking out of the room.

Chapter Twenty-Six

I 've never been more terrified than I am right now. Fear isn't something I'm accustomed to feeling, and it's not fear for myself. It's for her. I don't know where the fuck she is, and that's scaring the shit out of me.

She's reading my messages but hasn't replied. I

thought she just needed the night, that she'd be here this morning when I woke up. She wasn't, and I'm done giving her space. I can't afford to give it to her. Because I know if I do, I'll lose her for good. She'll come to her senses and realize I'm not good enough for her.

Fuck that. I'm not going to let that happen.

I grab my phone off the table next to me. I don't know anyone in this damn city besides my new teammates and I don't know them a whole lot either. Desperate times call for desperate measures, though, and that's why I press the green dial button next to his name.

"You still breathing?" Grayson asks as way of answering.

"I need a ride. Can you come get me?"

"Be there in twenty," he says, no questions asked. Just that he'll be here.

"I'll be out front."

"You breaking out, O'Neil?"

"Something like that." I pull myself up off the bed, and it's then that I notice I'm still wearing a fucking hospital gown. "I'm gonna need some clothes too," I add.

"Got it," he says before disconnecting the call.

My parents come into the room just as I sweep

my legs over the edge of the mattress. "What are you doing?" Mom asks.

"I need to get out of here," I tell her.

"You can't. Travis, you were shot."

"I've had worse injuries in youth league. I'm fine." It's a lie. My side hurts like a motherfucker, but I'm choosing to ride out the pain. Nothing is going to stop me from getting to Lili.

"Travis, you should lie down. Let me get the doctor," my father says.

"Dad, I need to go." I give him a pleading look.

He sighs and runs a hand through his hair. "Fine. Come on," he says as he wraps an arm around my waist and guides me to my feet.

"I can't believe you're just going to help him." Mom crosses her arms over her chest and pins my father with a glare.

"We either help him or he'll do it himself. It's your fault he's so damn stubborn, you know. The kid didn't get that trait from me," Dad says with a chuckle before turning back my way. "So, where exactly are we going?"

"Grayson is gonna pick me up out front. You and Mom should go to my place. There's not a lot there. We haven't furnished it yet but feel free to make yourselves at home. I can have whatever you need delivered," I tell him.

"You're aware you're wearing a dress, right?" Dad questions as we slowly shuffle over to the door.

"It's a hospital gown, not a dress, and I'm well aware," I grunt.

"Travis O'Neil, I just want you to know that I am fully against this plan of yours. Whatever it is. And when you make your injury worse, I'm going to be the one to say *I told you so*," Mom grumbles while holding the door open.

"Thanks, Mom. I promise. I really am fine." I'll be better once I get my eyes on Lili, but I don't say that part aloud.

By the time I make it to the front of the hospital, Grayson is leaning against his car waiting for me. He opens the passenger side door. "If you bleed on my leather, you're paying for the detail," he says as I fall into the seat.

"Worth it," I grunt as a sharp pain shoots through my body.

He jumps behind the wheel before glancing in my direction. "Where we going?"

"Take me to wherever the fuck Lili is," I tell him.

"Fuck. How did I know that's what you were going to say?" He shakes his head as his foot slams down on the accelerator. "She doesn't want to see you, you know."

"Yes, she does." I don't believe for an instant that Lili wants to leave me. If I did, I'd probably let her go.

Actually, no, I fucking wouldn't.

"It's your funeral." Grayson shrugs as he turns out of the parking lot.

My knuckles have barely made contact when the door is pulled open and an angry-looking Italian guy in a black suit glares at me. I don't wait for him to say anything as I step into the house.

"Lili, where are you?" I call out. And before I know it, my body is slammed up against the closest wall. My arm twisted behind my back.

"Who the fuck are you?" the guy asks. When I peer over my shoulder, I notice five more men just like him all pointing guns at my head.

"Told you... your funeral." Grayson laughs from the doorway.

"Get the fuck off me," I growl.

"Let him go." A commanding tone has me turning my head before my eyes connect with Lili's father.

"Fuck," I hiss out while clutching my side.

"Bullet wounds hurt like a bitch, huh?" Mr. Valentino says. "What are you doing here?"

"Where's Lili? I need to talk to her."

"If she wanted to see you, she would." Mr. Valentino folds his arms over his chest as he turns his glare on Gray. "Why the fuck did you bring him here?"

"He asked me to." Grayson shrugs his shoulders.

"Lili!" I call out again. Louder this time.

"Jesus-fucking-Christ, will you give the yelling a break?" Alessandro grunts from the stairs.

She's up there. I start to head in that direction when a hand lands on my chest. Stopping me. I look down. If the guy wasn't her brother and I didn't currently have a shit-ton of stitches in my body, I'd rip that fucking hand from his arm.

"I just want to talk to her," I tell him.

"She doesn't want to see you," Alessandro says.

"That's bullshit. She's running scared. It has nothing to do with her wanting to see me or not."

"You should tell them," Grayson hums from behind me.

I turn back to glare at him. "Shut the fuck up."

"Just saying. It'd make this a lot fucking easier if you did."

"Tell us what?" Mr. Valentino asks, but it's more like a command than a question.

I look around the room. There are a lot of ears, a lot of open spaces too. "Not here."

"This way." He turns down the hall without waiting for a reply.

I follow Alessandro into an office. Grayson strolls in behind me. I could be walking into a trap here. I have no idea who had me shot. Theoretically, Lili's father makes sense. But I don't see him doing that to her, no matter how much he might want to.

"What's going on?" Mr. Valentino asks while leaning against the desk, his hands shoved into the pockets of his trousers.

"Before I was shot, the guy said: *this is for Liliana.*"

Mr. Valentino's spine noticeably straightens. "Come again?"

"What the fuck?" Alessandro yells.

"I didn't exactly get to ask him questions," I remind them.

"He said those exact words?" Mr. Valentino attempts to clarify.

"Yes." I nod. "You can't tell her, though. She already thinks this is her fault. I will not have her blaming herself more than she is. I need her to believe that this had nothing to do with her."

Mr. Valentino and Alessandro have what sounds to be a heated conversation in Italian before the latter storms out of the room.

"Can I see her?"

Mr. Valentino looks at me for a long minute. "If you can make it up the stairs. Second door on your left," he grunts as he walks around the desk, picks up his phone, and brings it to his ear.

"Thank you."

Chapter Twenty-Seven

I startle awake. I swear I could hear Travis calling out for me at some point. I rub my hands over my face, the reality of my current situation sinking in with each second that passes.

I drag my ass out of the bed and walk into the bathroom. Turning on the hot water, I wait for the room to steam up before I strip off and get under the spray. I let the tears fall freely down my face as I slowly go through the motions of showering.

I need to find a way to stop this pain, to ease it even a little bit. Either that or learn to live with the constant ache, the emptiness I feel in the pit of my stomach. As my hands angrily swipe at my tears, I make a vow to never put myself in this position again.

Travis will forever be my person. No amount of distance between us will change that. He's just also the person I know I can't have. Not if I want him to live a full and happy life. And I do want that. More than anything, I want him to live. Because as much as I'm hurting now, as hard as it is to stay away from him, I know it'd be a thousand times worse if he died.

I turn off the shower, wrap a towel around my body, and grab another one from the shelf. After wiping my face, I run the towel over my hair, squeezing the water out of the ends before dropping it on the floor. I pick up my hair tie and pile the damp strands into a messy bun on top of my head. Then I walk out of the bathroom and over to the bag I left on the chair by the window. I make it halfway across the room when I stop and stare at the figure currently propped up on the bed.

I close my eyes and count to ten. When I open

them again, he's still there. I thought for sure I was seeing things. I take in every feature, every part of his body, before I make the mistake of meeting his gaze. Neither of us moves for what seems like an eternity until Travis slowly stands and takes a step towards me.

My hand shoots up. "Stop. Don't..." I shake my head. I cannot let him touch me. If I do, I don't know if I'll be strong enough to walk away from him again.

"Lili." His voice is low, and I can see the hurt in his eyes.

"I can't..." I swallow down the rest of my words. "Travis, what are you doing here? You should be in the hospital."

"No, where I should be is wherever you are, Lili."

"We can't... You should leave."

"I'm not leaving," he says. "We need to talk about this, Lili."

"There's nothing to talk about. It's not safe for you to be here, Travis. It's not safe for you to be with me. I'm not going to be the reason you die," I tell him.

"I didn't fucking die, Lili. I'm alive and well. Standing right here in front of you." He taps on his chest for emphasis.

"For how long? Until the next time? Travis, my

family... we have enemies. I should have known better than to let you get so close. And for that, I'm sorry."

"Bullshit. You're scared and I get it. I really do. But I will not let you fucking run from this. You and me, it's... I'm not giving you up," he says.

"You don't have a choice. You have to. You'll find someone else, Travis. You'll find a normal girl, with a normal family. And live a long, normal life." My stomach turns even as I say those words. I don't want him to find anyone else. I know that's completely irrational and selfish of me, though.

Travis laughs. It's a dark, hysterical kind of sound that lacks any actual humor. "You really want me to just move on? Go out there, find some other chick, and forget you ever existed?" His face screws up. Like just the thought makes him sick.

My mouth is dry, and my heart is beating out of my chest. "I don't see any other way for this to end. Not if I want you to keep breathing."

"That's awfully dramatic, babe," he says.

"It's the truth. Do you know how many funerals I've attended in my life?" I ask him.

"No," he says.

"Fifty-seven." I throw my hands in the air. "I've been to fifty-seven funerals, and I will not make yours fifty-eight. Because that'll be the one that ends me."

"That's not going to happen. You really think anything in this world is going to make me leave you, Lili? Not even *you* can prevent me from keeping you." Travis closes the gap between us.

"Please don't..." I ask him, my voice shaky.

"I love you, Lili. I love you so fucking much that I'm going out of my mind at the thought of losing you."

"I'm doing this *because* I love you, Travis," I attempt to explain.

"No, you're doing this because you're scared," he repeats.

"Of course I'm fucking scared!" I yell at him. "I got a phone call telling me you were shot while I was thousands of miles away. I had to look at you lying motionless in that hospital bed. I spent hours wondering if you were going to live, if you were going to wake up. So, yes, I'm scared. I'm fucking terrified. Of you dying. Of something happening to you that I can't control. Of losing you for good."

"You're not the only one who's scared here, Lili. I'm fucking terrified of losing you too. I can't. I won't. So whatever bullshit is going on in your head, get rid of it. You and me are end game. There is no other option. You say you want me to live, but I'm standing here telling you that I won't—*can't* live without you. I'm dying here, babe." He shakes his head. "How can I live without the one person in the world who makes me feel more alive than I ever have before? How can I live without the person who is my reason for living? That's you, in case you were wondering. You are mine, Liliana Valentino, and nothing is going to change that. Ever," he says.

My knees buckle. His closeness, his words... it's all too much. I fall to the ground as sobs rack my body. Travis curses as he follows me down. His arms close around me and he pulls me tight against his chest.

"Lili, you're breaking my fucking heart," he whispers.

"Better to be broken than buried," I reply through my tears.

"I disagree." His lips press onto my forehead. "I'd rather not live at all than live in a world where you're not mine."

"I'll always be yours," I tell him. "I just can't be *with* you."

Travis rocks me back and forth, his hands rubbing soothing circles along my spine. "I love you," he repeats over and over again.

"Sometimes love isn't enough, Travis. Love doesn't guarantee you a happy ending."

"Our love does. You'll see," he says.

"I just need space. I just need some time. I need to go home."

"Your home is here, with me."

"I'm sorry." I pull myself out of his arms. That's when I notice the blood seeping through his sweatshirt. "Travis, you're bleeding!" I shriek. "Shit. Oh my god." I jump to my feet, run to the door, and swing it open. "Alessandro, Enzo, Dad!" I list off every name I can think of.

"Lili, I'm fine," Travis grunts.

"You're not fine," I yell at him.

My dad and cousin come running up the stairs. With guns in their hands. Without a word, my father reaches out and throws me behind him.

"What the fuck?" he hisses when he peers into the room and sees Travis still on the bedroom floor.

"He's bleeding. Get a doctor," I tell him.

"Liliana, do not scream bloody murder when there's not an actual fucking *murderer* in the goddamn house," Dad huffs while holstering his weapon.

"Dad, he needs a doctor." I run back into the room and lift Travis's sweatshirt. I should have looked sooner. I should have found something to stop the bleeding.

"Is this all I had to do to get you to undress me, babe?" Travis looks at me with a smirk playing on his lips.

"You're an idiot. Also, my dad is right there," I whisper.

"He likes me."

"No, he doesn't. He doesn't like anyone whose name doesn't end with Valentino." I laugh.

"When we get married, you'll be an O'Neil. Bet he'll still love you then."

I stare at him. *When we get married?* I just told the man I can't be with him, that I need space, and he's talking about getting married.

"Doc's on the way," Enzo says.

"Thank you," I tell him.

Dad walks in with a first aid kit a few seconds later. "Liliana, go and get a wet towel."

I push to my feet and rush to the bathroom, running water over a towel before wringing it out. I watch in horror as red bleeds through the white of the fabric. There's blood on everything I touch. I need to remember that I've caused this. That Travis's blood is literally on my hands.

Chapter Twenty-Eight

I haven't taken my eyes off Lili. I don't know what she's thinking. Actually, I do. She's pulling away. I can feel it. And I need to figure out how to fucking stop her.

The doctor finishes applying new dressings and leaves the room. "You should be in bed," Lili says.

"This wouldn't have happened if you had just stayed in the hospital."

"And I would have stayed in the hospital, if my girlfriend were there with me," I tell her. Her father chuckles from where he's propped up by the door.

Lili glances in his direction before refocusing on me. "Where are your parents?"

"At our house."

She flinches. It's slight but I caught it.

"I'm sure they'd love to see you if you want to come home with me."

"Travis... I... I can't." Lili looks at me with so much sadness and despair in her eyes. I want to take it all away. I want those eyes to shine with nothing but happiness again. It fucking hurts seeing her like this.

"Don't do this," I plead with her. My hand shoots out to grip hers. I'm terrified of letting it go.

"I have to. Just... I'll get someone to take you home. I'll call you once I'm back in New York." Lili removes her hand from mine, and I feel like my whole world is slipping through my fingers.

I'm racking my mind, trying to figure out what to say, what could possibly break through her doubt right now, when she turns and walks out of the room.

Her father takes a step forward. "She just needs time," he says.

I blink at him. This man has wanted his daughter to leave my ass since the moment he met me. To the point he's put a gun to my head, attempting to scare me off more than once.

"How much time? Because I can't fathom a world without her." I know I'm spilling my guts to someone who couldn't give a fuck, but I'm at a loss as to what to do here.

"I've sent some guys over to your place. I'm increasing your security, and they're will be at least ten men on the grounds around the clock until I find the asshole who shot you."

"Why?" Truth is, I'm confused as to why her father would help me do anything.

"Because, despite what she says right now, my daughter loves you and I love her." He shrugs.

"I don't understand. If it wasn't your doing, who the fuck else would want to shoot me because of her?"

"I have no idea, but I'm going to fucking find out," he grunts, his teeth clenched and his jaw tight. "Until then, you both need to keep your heads low."

"I don't know how to go home without her," I admit.

"You don't have a choice—that's how. You need to give her the space she's asking for. She needs to work through her issues in her own way."

"You think she will?"

"Liliana can be stubborn, but I think she's going to come to the conclusion that she's better off with you than without you."

I nod my head. "Okay. Can you just...? She's going to be safe here, right?"

"I'm going to pretend you didn't just fucking ask me that," he growls at me. "My nephew will drive you home."

I walk into the house, my steps echoing off the walls as I enter. I haven't bothered to furnish it yet. I was waiting for Lili to make it a *home*.

"Nice place. Guess the NHL pays well." Enzo whistles as he looks around the foyer.

"I need your mother's number," I say as I pass him and head for the kitchen.

"What the fuck for?" he calls out after me.

"Lili mentioned your mom's an interior designer.

I want to see if she can get it done sooner rather than later." I pick up the bottle of Jack I left on the counter and raise it to my mouth.

Enzo swipes it out of my hands. "That's not a good idea. You're doped up on pain pills," he says before placing the bottle back on the counter.

"I don't care." I grit my teeth at him.

"I don't really give a shit if you kill yourself either, but my cousin will." He lifts one shoulder up and down. "I'll call Ma and let her know you want her services."

"Thank you."

"You need some fucking furniture." Enzo looks around the empty living space.

"Like I said, Lili wanted her aunt to decorate. I wasn't going to buy a bunch of shit just to have to throw it out later."

"You really do have it bad." Enzo laughs.

I roll my eyes. I'm past the point of caring who the fuck knows how I feel about this girl.

"Catch ya around. Oh, and do me a favor, would ya? Try not to die." Enzo waves a hand in the air as he walks back out the way we came in.

I manage to get up the stairs and to the bedroom. It's the only space that's furnished. Then I fall onto my bed and dig my phone out of my pocket. Ignoring all the missed calls and texts taking up my screen, I tap on Lili's name and type out a message.

ME:

I love you, Lili. Always. I don't care how long I have to wait. I will be here when you decide to come home.

SWEET LILI:

I love you too.

I read her reply over and over again. I don't doubt that she loves me. I know she does. But, fuck, her ability to push me away right now is messing with my head. Because all I want to do is pull her closer. I want to hold her and never let her go. I feel like my lungs are struggling to breathe, like I'm stuck underwater, and I'm drowning every second I'm not with her.

I'm about to tell her as much when my phone rings in my hand and my coach's number flashes across the screen.

"Coach?" I answer his call because I'm not a fucking idiot. If I don't, it'll be a lot worse later.

"Where the fuck are you, O'Neil? Because I'm at the hospital right now, and they're telling me you checked your ass out."

"I'm at home." I sigh.

"You're *at home?*" he yells down the line. "Against doctors' fucking orders?"

"I'm fine. I'll be back on the ice in no time."

"You won't be on the ice until you get clearance from the team doc," he huffs out. "If your ass isn't in a bed, I expect it to be warming the bench during practice tomorrow." Coach cuts the call without giving me a chance to respond.

Fuck me. Practice is the last thing I want to be thinking about right now.

I scroll through the rest of my notifications. I have three missed calls from my mom, and several more messages. I feel like shit for leaving my parents back at the hospital. I told them to come here but they chose to stay at the hotel instead.

I click on my mother's name and type out a reply.

ME:

I'm home. In bed. I'm good. Sorry, Mom. I'll call you tomorrow.

MOM:

Is Liliana with you?

ME:

No, she's staying at a rental house with her family.

MOM:

I'm sorry, Travis. I'm coming around with food.

ME:

I'm going to bed, Mom. I'll call you tomorrow.

MOM:

Okay.

I don't for one second believe she's taking no for an answer, though. She'll head over now that she knows I'm home. I don't want to be an asshole, but I'm fucking exhausted and not in the mood to deal with people.

Unless that person is Lili. I'd gladly fucking deal with her if only she'd let me.

Chapter Twenty-Nine

Liliana

The commotion coming from downstairs has me actually leaving the bedroom I've been holed up in for the past two days. I asked my dad to take me home, and he said he would... after he works out a few things here. What business he could possibly have in Vancouver, I have no idea. But I'm smart enough not to ask him questions. It's not like he'd tell me anyway. He's always vague about what he actually does, and now that he's the Don, well, he's even more tight-lipped than before.

I stop in my tracks when I find all of my uncles, along with my cousins Dante and Orlando, positioned around the living room.

"What are you all doing here?" I ask my uncles before pointing to my cousins. "And shouldn't you two be in school?"

Dante shrugs. "*He* should be. I don't need to be there. It's not like those teachers can actually teach me anything I don't already know," he says with an arrogant smirk on his face. The kid is a genius. There's no denying that, but sometimes I think his ego needs to be knocked down a peg or two.

"Where's Josie?" I ask. He's never too far from his girlfriend, who's also my newly adopted sister.

Dante sends my father a look that tells me he's none too happy to be without her. "At home."

"You mean you left her? In New York? All by herself? Shit, Dante, didn't she tell you about the two guys currently vying for her attention at school?" I raise a hand to my chest with feigned concern.

Dante scoffs. "As if anyone would dare to even try to talk to her."

I shake my head as a smirk curls my lips. "Sisters gossip about boys, you know. She tells me things she'd never tell you." It's a lie. I'm totally trying to get under his skin, and judging by the scowl on his face, it's working.

Dante storms out of the living room while tapping on his phone. I watch him go before turning my focus on Orlando.

"You ain't got shit on me, coz." He laughs and spreads himself out wider on the sofa.

"Why are you all here? What's going on?"

"Can't I just come to see my favorite niece?" Zio Matteo asks, walking over and pulling me into a hug.

"You can, but Tilly isn't here." I laugh.

"Ouch, Liliana, you wound me. You know you're my favorite little heir," he says. My uncles like to call all of us kids their *little heirs*.

"Sure I am. But don't try to get out of answering my question. What's going on?" I repeat more forcefully this time. Like I said before, I'm not fucking stupid, and the fact that everyone has gathered in one place tells me something big is happening.

"Well, I'm not sure if you're aware, but your little boyfriend got shot, Lil. We're here to find out who did it," Zio Romeo chimes in, and a sharp pain tears through my chest. Like my heart is physically breaking in two.

I bring up a hand and rub the spot, but it does nothing to dull the ache. "He's not my boyfriend."

"Does he know that?" Zio Luca lifts a challenging brow while gesturing to the other side of the room, where there are dozens and dozens of floral arrangements sprawled out on every surface.

I walk over and pull out a card from the closest one.

This lifetime and into the next, I'll be waiting for you. I love you.
—Travis

My hand shakes as I set the card down. Then I take in a lungful of air, trying to calm my racked nerves. "It doesn't matter. When you find out who shot him, I want to know." I look directly at my father, and something flashes in his eyes.

"I'll let you know after we've dealt with them," he says.

"*Before* would be preferred." I cross my arms over my chest.

"That's not fucking happening, Liliana. You are not touching this," he growls. My father has always been insistent that I don't follow the rest of them down *that* path. That I not venture into the criminal underworld side of the business.

Right now, though, I can't think of anything else I'd rather do than show them all what I'm made of. I am a Valentino after all, and someone just tried to take out the person I love. I've sat around and cried about it for long enough. I'll let them find the guy, but I'm determined to be the one to show that person what happens when you cross us. Or at least be in the room when it happens. I might not be able to pull that trigger when it comes down to it, but I can watch. Of that much, I'm certain.

I walk out of the room without another word. There is no point arguing about it now. I'll wait until after they've found the guy.

The day has dragged by. Travis has messaged me a million times. So has Gray, who was kind enough to send me a photo of Travis sitting on the bench during their morning skate. He looked awful. Even from the blurry photo, I could see how much he was hurting. His eyes were lacking their usual spark, his posture deflated. But his heart is still beating. That's what I need to keep reminding myself.

The pain I'm causing both of us isn't for nothing. It has a purpose. That knowledge doesn't make it any easier to keep ignoring his messages, though. With each new one that pops up, I feel myself closer to breaking the silence and calling him, telling him to come and get me. Take me home.

The hushed voices flittering from the kitchen have me stopping and pressing myself against the wall before I walk in. I recognize one of the men as Grayson's father, Jacob Monroe. The guy runs the criminal underground in Vancouver—actually in all of Canada. He's also the owner of the Knights, Travis's dream team.

"I need to find out who did this. Someone has a hard-on for my daughter, Jacob, and I won't leave without their heads in a fucking bag," my father growls.

My brows furrow. *What is he talking about?*

"I know, and we will find them. But until that happens, you can't just go around burning my city to the fucking ground," Mr. Monroe says.

"And who's going to stop me? You?" Dad laughs.

"I'm not your enemy here, Valentino. All we know is that whoever shot Travis mentioned something about it being for Liliana. We have nothing else to go on. The kid's got no description, and the CCTV was cut for a whole hour. Whoever did this knows what they're doing. We need to figure out the why, and maybe that'll lead us to the who."

My hand comes up to cover my mouth. Travis was shot because of me. I called it. It's the reason I have to push him away. It's the reason I can't be weak and cave to my need to be with him. But if it wasn't my father who ordered the hit, then who the hell was it?

Chapter Thirty

I t's been a week. A long-ass fucking week without Lili. I've tried to talk to her. I've tried and failed to give her the space she wants. I'll keep calling and messaging her until she decides to talk to me. Even if it's just to tell me to fuck off and leave her alone. At this point, I'd take anything if it means getting a response from her.

I've heard from Grayson that she's still in Vancouver. She didn't return to New York like she planned. She's with her family, and according to him, the whole tribe is here. I've had a few visits from her brother and cousins. I think they're on some kind of rotating roster, checking that I'm still alive. They've tried to not make it obvious, but it is. I couldn't give a fuck about myself, though. I'm worried about her. It's always her.

She's on my mind constantly. Even now, as I sit on the bench in the locker room, watching my teammates get ready to play the first preseason game, I can't stop thinking about her. Don't get me wrong... I'm fucking pissed as hell that I'm benched. This isn't exactly how I pictured my first game with the Knights going.

I pull out my phone and text Lili for the millionth time.

ME:

> Is it weird that I'm more worried about you and what you're doing than what I'm having to do right now?

I see the read notice on the message, and then

the three little dots pop up, indicating she's typing a reply.

SWEET LILI:

What are you doing?

ME:

About to sit out my first Knights game.

SWEET LILI:

I'm sorry. I know how much you love being out there. What have the doctors said? When will you be back on the ice?

This is the most she's spoken to me in a week. And I'll do anything I can to keep her talking. Which means I'm overthinking my reply. I don't want to scare her off.

ME:

I love you more than hockey, Liliana. I hate sitting on the bench, but I hate going to bed at night without you more. I hate waking up and not seeing your beautiful face.

ME:

Doctors are saying two months.

SWEET LILI:

I hate it too.

That's it. Just... *I hate it too.*

Fuck, my hand clenches around the phone. I know she loves me. I know she's scared that her family connections will impact me. But she doesn't get that living without her isn't fucking living at all.

ME:

Then come home.

SWEET LILI:

You know I can't do that, Travis. I can't be the reason you get hurt again.

I don't tell her that right now she is the exact reason I'm hurting. I don't tell her that I'm breaking down without her.

ME:

This isn't your fault, Lili. I love you.

I tuck my phone away and follow my teammates out through the tunnel. My parents are in the stands. I told them they could go home, that they didn't need to be here tonight. I'm not even playing. They refused, saying that whether I was on the ice or not, this was my first game as a Knight, and that they were not missing it.

I sit down and look out to the crowd. Something

has me glancing up at the boxes. Where the Monroes usually get together to watch the game. And I can't look away. She's here. Staring right back at me. Lili is standing between her father and Gray's sister. I pull my phone out of my pocket.

ME:
You're here.

SWEET LILI:
I wasn't going to miss your first game as a Knight.

ME:
Come down to the tunnel.

The little dots pop up on the screen before they're gone again. I watch Lili turn to Aliyah and then step away from the window. Fuck, I fucking scared her off.

I run my hands through my hair. I'm so fucking frustrated. I feel out of control, out of my depths when it comes to her. I keep telling myself that I just have to be patient. That she'll come to her senses. I know she will. I have to believe that. Because the alternative—the idea that I've lost her forever—isn't something I can live with.

I try to turn my attention back on the ice. I should be cheering on my teammates. I should be focused on the game. Hockey used to be the love of my life. I honestly never thought anything could top it. Until I met Lili.

At the end of the first period, I get up and walk down the tunnel before the rest of the team is even off the ice. I stop dead in my tracks when I get to the locker room and Lili is standing with Aliyah just outside the door. I stare at her. Frozen to the spot. Almost too scared to move an inch and risk her running off.

"Hey." Lili gives me a sad smile.

"Hi." The rest of the guys make their way inside the locker room—well, everyone except King. He stops and scoops Aliyah into his arms and spins her around.

She reaches out a hand to swat at his chest. "Ew, put me down. You're all sweaty."

"You love it when I'm sweaty." King grins and earns himself a slap upside the back of his head from Gray.

"That's my fucking sister, dick."

"I'm well aware," King replies before setting Aliyah back on her feet and following Grayson into the locker room.

I wait until everyone is gone before I speak again. "That's a good look," I tell Lili. She's wearing my

Knights jersey. Seeing my number on her is always the biggest fucking turn-on.

"Thanks. I couldn't *not* support the best player on the team," she says.

"I heard that, Lil," Grayson yells out from the locker room.

I take a step towards her. "Thanks for coming."

"My dad forced me... It's not that I didn't want to be here. I just didn't want to complicate things," she says.

I reach out and grab hold of her hand. Such a simple fucking touch. Yet the instant my skin makes contact with hers, I feel a strong sense of peace wash over me. Like I've just come home after being away for a long time.

"I've missed you so fucking much," I whisper and pull her against me.

She's tense for a moment before I feel her body relax and lean into mine. Her arms close around my waist. "I'm so sorry. I wish things could be different. I really do," she says.

"They can be, Lili. The only people who get to decide our fate are us. You and me. That's all that matters. As long as we're together, we can overcome anything." I kiss the top of her head.

"I wish it were that simple." Lili pulls away from

me, and I can feel her trying to put distance between us in more ways than one.

"Tell me that you don't love me... Tell me you don't love me and I'll stop fighting for us." It's a lie. I'm never going to stop fighting. But she doesn't need to know that.

"I can't..." She shakes her head and drops her eyes to the ground.

"Then I'm going to keep fighting for us. I will never stop." I tip her chin up and force her to look at me.

"I have to go. I'm sorry. I shouldn't have come down here. I just wanted to... I needed to see you," she admits.

"You should stay. You can watch the game from the bench with me." I lift a shoulder in a half-shrug. Pretending like it's no big deal.

"I can't," she repeats. And without another word, Lili turns and walks away. It's only then that I notice the two bulking men in black suits trailing behind her. I was so wrapped up in seeing her I didn't notice anyone was even watching us.

Chapter Thirty-One

I should not have gone to the game last night. I wanted to be there for Travis. I was hoping to be there for him *without* his knowledge, though. When my father handed me a jersey, told me to put it on, that we were going to the game, I couldn't argue with him. Not after I had been fighting with myself about it all day.

I definitely should not have gone to the locker room, and I should not have let Travis hold me the way he did. I wanted to fall against him and never let go. I wanted to fuse myself to him, sink into how safe I always feel in his arms.

I can't do that. I can't risk his safety. My head is so messed up right now. I have no idea what the right thing to do is anymore.

I pick up the phone, scroll to my group chat with my cousins Tilly and Aurora, and hit the video call icon. Maybe they can talk some sense into me—well, maybe Tilly can at least. She's the smart, sensible one. Not that Aurora isn't smart. She just doesn't use her brains for anything good.

"Hey, stranger, how's Canada?" Tilly picks up first.

"Cold. How are things at home?" I ask, my heart aching a little when I mention the word.

Home. This city was supposed to become my new home. I was supposed to start a life with Travis here. And now, I have no idea what I'm going to do. I quit my job in New York. I had interviews lined up with advertising agencies all next week.

"Quiet, considering everyone is in Vancouver with you," Tilly says.

"Bitch, why has it taken you this long to call?" Aurora enters the chat with her usual bravado.

"Sorry... I've been...Well, I've been... you know?" I shrug.

"What happened? Who do I need to make disappear?" she asks.

"No one," I tell her.

"How's Travis?" Tilly chimes in.

"He said it'll be another two months or so before he can play again."

"But how is he?" Tilly presses. I look at Aurora, and she's staring right back at me, scrutinizing my every feature.

"I broke up with him," I whisper.

"Why on this God-given earth would you break up with that man? Have you seen him? Shit, Lil, he's insanely hot. And I can tell by the way he moves on the ice that he fucks well. So, again, why the fuck did you break up with him?" Aurora lifts a challenging brow. "Unless he did something to hurt you?"

I know what she's doing. She's baiting me. Waiting to see if I'll react. But I'm too exhausted to play into it. "He was shot, Aurora. Because of me," I tell her. "I can't be with him and risk it being what gets him killed."

"Bullshit. That's the stupidest thing I've ever heard. Tilly, you're the smart one. Tell her that's stupid."

"First of all, I'm not the smart one. You're both very intelligent. And secondly, for once, I agree with her, Lil. That was stupid. It's not a reason to break up with someone," Tilly says.

"Keeping him safe isn't stupid. I could never live with myself if anything else were to happen to him because of me." I sigh.

"Why do you keep insisting it had anything to do with you in the first place? Wasn't that King guy shot not all that long ago? That had nothing to do with you."

"I overheard Dad and Mr. Monroe talking, and they said that whoever shot Travis told him it was for me. Because of me."

The girls let out a collective gasp. "Wait, but I thought your dad had nothing to do with it?" Aurora asks, and I shrug.

"He didn't."

"So who was it then? Who on earth would have a reason to shoot Travis *for you*?" Tilly questions.

"I don't know." I shake my head. "I've been

trying to figure that out. I have no idea. And no one else is any closer to finding out who it was either."

"I'm so sorry, Lil." Tilly wipes at her face. She's always been emotional—the girl cries over a tissue commercial. While I appreciate all the work that goes into a good advertisement, that's a little much... even for me.

"Don't cry. You'll make me cry, and I've cried enough this week," I tell her.

"Well, I still think breaking up with Travis was a bullshit move. If you ask me, you should be with him. Help the guy mend. Sponge baths and all that." Aurora waves a hand in the air with a devilish smirk on her face. I laugh when she begins fanning herself.

"I'm sorry, Lil. I have to go. Class is about to start." Tilly looks around, and it's only now that I notice she's in a lecture hall.

"Thanks for chatting. I have to get up and drag my ass out of bed anyway," I huff.

"We'll talk again soon," Aurora says, disconnecting the chat first.

"I'm really sorry, Lil. You should follow whatever your heart tells you to do. If it wants you to be with Travis, then go to him. If it doesn't, then come home and we can get drunk."

"Thanks, Tilly."

The screen goes blank and I lie back down on the pillow. I don't know how long I stare at the ceiling, but eventually the rumbling of my stomach has me crawling out of bed.

"What are you doing here? And what the fuck happened to your head?" Zio Matteo calls out from the foyer.

"I'm here because my cousin needs me. And I dyed my hair because Zia Izzy said blondes have more fun. She was right by the way," Aurora replies, smirking while she pops a piece of chewing gum into her mouth. "I've been having all sorts of... fun."

I run down the hall as soon as I hear her voice. "Aurora?" I just spoke to her this morning and now she's here. My cousin shoves past her father, rushes over to me, and wraps her arms around my neck. She squeezes me tight. A little *too tight*.

"I can't breathe," I tell her.

"Sorry. I just missed you," she says as she pulls back.

I reach out and run my fingers through her hair. "I love it."

"Right? So do I," Aurora says and then turns to her father. "I look good, right, Daddy?"

"You always look beautiful, Aurora. You don't need to be blonde to accomplish that," he grinds out.

"Ma's blonde," Aurora reminds him.

"Your mother is a natural blonde," he counters. "And stop trying to change the subject. How did you get here?"

"I took a flight. First class, of course. It's not the same as the jet, but it wasn't bad, I guess." Aurora smiles.

"By yourself?"

"Yep, all by myself. Who would have thought little ol' me was capable of such a thing?" Aurora rolls her eyes before she grabs my hand. "Come on, we have so much to catch up on," she says as she drags me back up the stairs.

"Aurora, we're not done talking about this," Zio Matteo calls after her.

"Okay, Daddy. I'll come find you after I'm done with Lil."

I turn and offer my uncle a weak smile, and he just shakes his head at us.

Once we're closed inside the bedroom, Aurora

turns to me with a wicked grin on her face. "Okay, we're going to plan how to get that boy back," she says.

"No, we're not. And there is nothing boyish about Travis O'Neil—trust me."

"Yes, we are. You're miserable as hell and I am not going to sit by and watch you hurt yourself because you're all stuck in your own head."

"Aurora, it's not that simple." I force out a long sigh and flop onto the bed. "He got shot because of me."

"You know Zio Luca jumped in front of a bullet for Zia Katy, right? And they're doing just fine."

"That's different."

"How?"

"Zio Luca was part of the life. He knew the risks. And besides, he's always getting shot. It wasn't anything new to him."

"He was a football player when he jumped in front of that bullet. I've watched some of the news clips. He was a hero, really. But that's not the point. The point is... Travis got shot, but he survived, Lil, and you're over here acting like the guy is dead."

"No, trust me, I would not be functioning if he actually died." I shake my head.

"Your hair looks like you haven't washed it for a

week, and you have the darkest bags under your eyes. But, sure, let's pretend everything is just fine," she says while gesturing to my face.

"Thanks a lot." I shove at her shoulder.

"You know I love you, but I'm going to be honest when I think you're being an idiot. You love him. He loves you. The end." Aurora claps her hands together. Like that's it. Like it's a done deal.

I wish it were that simple. I wish love was enough to overcome everything. But it's not.

"You're being a martyr because you're scared of getting hurt. But here's the thing, coz... You're a Valentino. We do not run from anything. We look our fears in the eye and suffocate it. What we don't do is give it the freedom to grow and smother us."

I look at her and snort. "Who gave you that little bit of wisdom?"

"Nonno." She smiles. "And he's right. No one is scarier than Nonno," she says. "Well, except maybe Zio Theo. Your dad is on the same level."

"He is." I laugh.

Is she right, though? Am I only running from what Travis and I have because I'm scared? I know I'm terrified of something happening to him, of losing him forever. And pushing him away... well, that's practically the same thing. Either way, I don't have him in my life anymore.

Chapter Thirty-Two

The doorbell rings through the house, with a constant repeating chime. They won't stop pressing the buzzer. I roll my eyes, making no effort to rush to invite them in. Whoever it is, I know they're a *Valentino-approved* guest. If they weren't, the men Lili's father has surrounding my place would have prevented them from even making it to the front door.

At first, I wanted to refuse his help. Tell Mr. Valentino they all had to go. That I don't need his protection. The only reason I didn't is because he's Lili's father, and for once, the guy isn't threatening to kill me. Instead, he's my only real form of contact with her, the only one who answers when I ask how she's doing a million times a day.

I pull the door open and frown. "What the fuck are you all doing here?" I ask Grayson, who is the first one to barge past me and help himself into my house. He's closely followed by Liam King and Luke Jameson, my new teammates. Then Lili's brother and one of her numerous cousins—Enzo, I think.

"Drinking our sorrows away," Liam replies with a smirk while holding up a six-pack.

"You're going to need more than that to drink your sorrows away, King. You're about to have Monroe for a brother-in-law." I laugh, even though I don't feel like laughing. And I sure as shit don't feel like entertaining these assholes right now either.

"Fuck off. Have you seen the family you're marrying into, fucker?" Grayson throws out an arm towards Alessandro and Enzo.

My heart fucking aches at the thought of Lili. I

couldn't give a shit who her family is. I would marry that girl tomorrow if she'd let me. That thought has me frozen to the spot.

Would she let me? Would she say *no* if I asked her?

"Who the fuck says they're getting married? I didn't see no ring on my sister's finger," Alessandro grunts.

"Yet," I tell him. "But there will be."

"Good luck with that. She won't even talk to you right now." Enzo laughs. I glare at him, which only causes him to laugh harder.

"Again, why the fuck are you all here?" I look at each of the guys currently filling my otherwise empty foyer.

"Drinking," Luke says. "It's our day off and we won last night. So we're drinking."

I don't tell him that I didn't even play. That I didn't win shit. The team did great, sure, but when you did fuck all to contribute to that game, you can't really claim the glory.

"I'm not in the mood," I huff.

"Too bad. We're drinking. His little sister just arrived in town, which means sometime within the next twelve hours, we're going to have to bail her out of some fucked-up shit she managed to get herself into. And I, for one, need a shit-ton of alcohol for that," Alessandro says, pointing at Enzo.

"Fuck you. My sister is an angel." Enzo defends, although you can tell he doesn't believe a word of it.

"No, *my sister* is an angel. Yours is the devil in female form." Alessandro laughs.

"Your sister really *is* a fucking angel," I agree. Because I'm certain Lili fell from heaven and I was the one lucky enough to catch her. "Come on. If we're drinking, I want the good stuff." I walk through the house and into the kitchen, where I have a few bottles of whiskey lined up on the counter.

I scoop them up, along with glasses my mom went out and bought. She stocked the kitchen with supplies, saying that I couldn't live in a completely empty house. I disagree. I could live this way forever if I had to. Without Lili, I don't see the point of having anything else.

After pouring a glass for each of us, I pull my phone out of my pocket and check my messages. I don't know why I keep doing this. She hasn't messaged back. She won't. My fingers start tapping on the screen anyway and I press send before I can stop myself.

ME:

> How likely are your brother and cousin to fuck up our house if their asses get drunk here?

She reads my text and then my phone lights up with her picture. She's calling me. I smile. I had a feeling that would finally get a response from her.

"I'll be back. Don't break anything," I say to my... friends? Teammates? Future in-laws? Whoever the fuck they are. Then I click the answer button on my phone. "Hey."

"Why are Alessandro and Enzo at your house?" Lili asks me.

"Our house, babe. They're at *our* house," I correct her. "And I have no idea. They just showed up with Grayson, Liam, and Luke. Apparently, they're here to drink *my* sorrows away."

"Is that wise? For you to be drinking?"

"Well, it sure as shit ain't going to help my sorrows. The only thing that could do that is you coming home," I tell her.

"Travis, I..."

"I know... *You can't.*" I sigh into the phone. I'm trying really fucking hard to be patient with her. I'm doing my best not to lose my shit. But, fuck, I just want to scream. Barge into that rental house and force her to come home.

"I'll tell Alessandro to leave," she says. "I'm sorry. They shouldn't be bothering you."

"Don't do that. They're fine. Besides, what better time to get to know my future in-laws?"

I hear the hitch in her breath. Then she goes deadly silent.

"Lili?"

"I'm so sorry. I know I'm messing everything up. I'm trying to do the right thing here, Travis."

"The right thing for you to do is to come home, Lili. We can work out the rest later," I tell her. "Please, just come home."

"I have to go," she says and the line goes dead.

"Fuck!" I throw my phone at the wall.

"Didn't you just tell us not to break shit?"

I turn at the sound of Alessandro's voice. He's leaning against the wall with his hands in his pockets. "It's my house. I'll break whatever the fuck I want," I grit out. My fists open and close at my sides.

"Sure, go ahead and trash the joint. Just make sure I'm here when Lili sees what you've done to it. I want to hear the lecture she gives you." He chuckles.

"Well, she's not fucking here. And I really don't know if she ever will be." I toss my hands in the air.

"She will," he says.

"How can you be so sure?"

"Because I know my sister, and I know that she loves you. She will come around."

"When? Is there like some kind of manual I missed? Because I'd really like to fucking know when I can expect my girlfriend back."

"A manual? That would have made growing up with the girl a lot fucking easier. Especially during her teenage years—man, was she moody." He laughs. "Come on. Let's get a drink. There isn't anything you can do right now except give her the space she's asking for."

"That's a lot easier said than done."

"She's still here, isn't she? Ma wanted her to fly back to New York and Lil refused. The only thing keeping her in Vancouver is you."

"Any news on the shooter?" I ask him.

"Not yet. The guy's a fucking ghost. But that's fine. 'Cause we happen to be the best fucking ghost hunters there are."

When we walk back into the kitchen, Grayson is on the phone. He has the call on speaker and he's laughing. Like something's funny. I freeze to the spot when whoever's on the other end starts talking again.

I reach out and grab Alessandro's hand. "That's him," I say, keeping my voice low.

"Who?"

"That guy, on the phone. That's the fucker who shot me." I take a step forward, ready to pick up the phone and read the name or number on the screen, when Alessandro's hand lands on my chest. Stopping my movements.

"Don't say a fucking word." He glances over his shoulder and then turns back to me. "How sure are you?"

"Fucking certain."

"Fuck." He runs a hand through his hair. "Okay. I need you to stay here. Act like you don't know shit. Do not let Monroe in on a single fucking thing. You got me?"

"Who is it?"

"Doesn't matter. We'll handle it. My pops and I," Alessandro assures me. "I need you to stay here and keep up appearances. We cannot let this fucker know we're on to him."

"Okay." I nod my head. There isn't anything I wouldn't do to protect Lili. Whoever this asshole is, he wants something from her. *That* I'm sure of.

"Enzo, we gotta go. It took less than thirty

minutes for that sister of yours to fuck up." Alessandro calls out to his cousin.

Enzo straightens. "What'd she do?"

"I'll tell you in the car. Let's go." Alessandro doesn't wait for a response before he makes his way back to the front door.

"Guess the party just got smaller," I say while reaching out and swiping up the bottle of whiskey. I refill the empty glasses. I'd much rather be out there hunting the fucker down. But if this is what I have to do to get the guy, so be it.

Chapter Thirty-Three

Travis has been texting me nonstop. I've replied to some of his messages. But others, I choose not to. It's hard. Every fiber of my being wants to be with him. But my need to keep him out of my family's business is just as strong.

My heart and mind are at war with each other, and at this point, I don't know which one is going to win. Aurora made me write a pro-and-con list. The pro side was long, while there was only one con I could think of. The risk to his safety.

My whole family seems to be on Team Travis at the moment too. Even my father, who is acting like he's got a new best friend. It's weird. I don't know how to begin to unpack that relationship. My father has been vehemently against me dating anyone. And now, all of a sudden, he's Travis's biggest cheerleader. Telling me that I should talk to him. That I should listen to him.

I wish it were that simple. If it were, I'd be with Travis right now instead of lying awake in this bed. My own thoughts making me crazy and an overwhelming need to go and see him eating at me. I roll over. Aurora is next to me. We both fell asleep in here last night while watching a rom-com I can't even remember the name of.

"Aurora, are you awake?" I whisper.

"Argh, if you're not dead or dying, you're about to be," she mumbles back.

"Wanna sneak out?"

Her eyes pop open and a devious smirk curls her

lips. "I thought you'd never ask," she says. "Where we going?"

"The rink. I know they have practice soon, and I want to see Travis," I tell her.

"About damn time. Okay, let's do this." She's out of bed and getting dressed before I can come up with a reason to change my mind. This is why I love my cousin so much. She's prepared to do anything for me.

I shove the blankets aside and get out of bed. Digging through my bag, I pull out a pair of jeans and a sweater. I quickly apply the smallest bit of makeup on my face. Because, well, I'm about to see Travis. I have no idea what I'm going to say to him, or if I'll say anything at all. Right now, I just want to see him.

"Okay, I clocked eight out front, four on the right, and three on the left. Then there's ten more at the back," Aurora says. "It seems excessive, even for Zio Theo."

She's right. There are a lot of my father's men keeping watch, double what was here two days ago. "Something is going on... Something they're not telling us about," I say.

"Isn't there always?"

"We're not going to be able to sneak out." I sigh.

"Where there's a will, there's always a way." Aurora smirks.

"I'm going to wake my brother up. He'll take us out, and the guards won't even question it," I tell her.

"That *would* be the easy way to do things— although I'm all for the sneaking past them too."

"Come on." I open the bedroom door, and sure enough, there are two guards in the hallway. They immediately look up when we walk out. I smile as I pass them and enter my brother's room. The minute I lean on his bed, Alessandro rolls over and points a pistol at me.

"What the fuck, Liliana? Are you trying to get yourself killed?" he grunts as he drops the gun back down on the mattress.

My head tips to the side as I look at him. "Do you always sleep with a gun in your hand? That cannot be safe, Alessandro."

"It's fine. And it wasn't in my hand. It was under my pillow."

I actually hate that he feels like he has to sleep like this. Maybe me going to see Travis is a horrible idea.

"What's wrong?" Alessandro asks.

"I... ah..."

"She wants to go see lover boy, and obviously we

can't break out of Fort Knox without you," Aurora says.

My brother looks at me as he takes hold of my hand. "You want to go see Travis?"

I nod my head. "I think so."

"You think or *you know*. Because I gotta be honest, Lil, you can't go there and see him and then walk away again. The dude has more patience than Mother Teresa when it comes to you, but even he has a breaking point."

My mouth drops into a frown. "You're supposed to be on my side."

"I am *always* on your side, Lil. You're my sister, but I'm telling you Travis is struggling with the fact that you're not talking to him."

"I know." I can admit that I've done this to us, even if my intentions were to keep him safe.

"Okay, I'll take you. But you might want to wait in the hall so I can get up. Unless you want to get an eyeful of my junk."

"Ew, that's disgusting." I jump off my brother's bed quicker than I've ever moved in my life.

My hands shake with nerves as we follow Grayson into the rink. I messaged him when we were in the car, telling him I was stopping by and to open the door for me.

"You owe me twenty K, Valentino," Gray says to my brother.

"You don't know that yet," Alessandro argues. His hand finds mine and he grips it tight to stop it from shaking. I look up and he gives me the slightest reassuring smile.

"She's here. I win." Gray crosses his arms over his large chest.

"You win what?" I ask, my eyes bouncing between him and my brother.

"Nothing," Alessandro and Gray say at the same time.

"Bullshit." Aurora glares at them. "You guys were betting on her? What was it? And don't think I'll spare you just because you're blood." She points a finger at Alessandro, who winces.

"Like I said, it's nothing. We just had a discussion about how long it was going to take Lil to come to her senses." Alessandro shrugs. I try to slip my hand out of his grip, but he holds it tighter. "Come on, let's go find this boyfriend/not boyfriend of yours," he says.

"Wait! I need to use the restroom first," I mutter as I tug my arm free.

"There, just down the hall." Gray points behind us.

"I'll be right back," I tell them.

"I'll come with you." Aurora starts walking next to me.

"I'll be right back. I just need a minute," I tell her.

"Okay, I'll wait here then."

I rush inside the bathroom, turn on the faucet, pull the sleeves of my sweater up, and splash the water on my forearms. I don't know why I'm so nervous. It's Travis. I can see him, talk to him without feeling so out of sorts.

The door to the restroom opens behind me.

"Aurora, I'm fine," I call out. There's no answer, but there is the sound of heavy footsteps echoing off the walls. I look up into the mirror and jump out of my skin before turning around. "What are you doing in here?"

"I've been waiting for you, Liliana."

"Why?" I flick my eyes to the doorway. I'd have to get around him to make it there. If I scream, will Alessandro or Gray be able to hear me?

"I wouldn't." Lou Monroe takes a step closer and then another.

"What do you want?" I ask while trying to keep my voice calm. I've never liked the guy. On the few occasions when I've interacted with Gray's uncle, he's always creeped me out. But right now, my fight-or-flight instincts are at an all-time high.

I don't see his hand swipe out, or the needle he stabs into my skin before he closes his arms around my waist. "Sorry, but it's going to be easier this way," he says, holding me upright.

"What?" I can hear my words slurring as my limbs start to go numb. Then the room is spinning, my bag drops to the ground, and everything goes black.

Chapter Thirty-Four

"What are you all doing here?" I direct my question to Alessandro. I just walked into the rink for morning skate, not that I'll be doing any actual skating.

"Lil wanted to come see you," he says.

"She's here? Where?" My heart races. *She's here. She wants to see me.*

"She just went to the restroom." Lili's cousin Aurora points down the hall, and I'm walking that way before she can finish speaking.

I push through the door marked *female* and call out, "Lili?"

By the time I make it all the way inside the bathroom, it's clear no one else is here. I'm about to turn around and walk out when I see something on the ground. Bending down, I pick up a handbag. Not just any handbag. Lili's. I know this because she spent an hour talking to me about the thing before she bought it.

"Lili?" I call out again, louder this time, as I push inside every stall even though I already know they're empty. "Fuck!" Ignoring the searing pain in my side, I run back out to where Grayson and Alessandro are waiting. "Where the fuck is she?" I glance around, my eyes scanning the ice, the stands, everywhere I can see. "Lili!"

Without a word, Aurora and Alessandro rush past me and into the bathroom. She's not there. She's supposed to be there and she's not.

"Fuck." I turn to Grayson and throw my arms in his direction. "Do something. Find her."

He's on his phone and running across the arena. Away from the bathrooms. I don't know what to do. She can't be far. How long was she in there by herself?

I jog down the hallway, yelling out her name, and eventually push through the back door that leads to the parking lot. I turn when I hear footsteps behind me. Alessandro. "Where the fuck is she?" I scream at him.

He looks at me, his face a stony mixture of desperation, fear, and anger. Aurora comes out behind him. "I'm calling the boss," she says.

"I'll do it. Go and find Gray. I want all the CCTV footage. Everything," he tells her. She doesn't wait before she runs back into the building.

My lungs fight for air. Someone took Lili. Someone has her and is doing God knows what with her. My stomach twists into a knot.

"Fuck! Is her phone in there?" Alessandro points to the handbag still clutched to my chest.

I open the bag and dig through the contents. "No phone," I tell him. But I do feel the outline of a hand-gun. She was taken and she doesn't even have a way to protect herself.

"Good. Hopefully she has it with her," he says as

he pulls his own phone to his ear. "Pops... Lil... she... fuck!" Alessandro tugs at his hair.

"Where the fuck are you?" I hear her father's voice shout down the line.

"The rink. She went to the bathroom. She's... someone took her."

"What the fuck do you mean someone took her, Alessandro? How the fuck could you let that happen on your watch?"

"I..." Alessandro looks to me with a desperation I've never seen in his eyes before.

"I'm on my way. Find that fucker Monroe right now."

"Monroe?" I parrot while looking at Alessandro.

"Lou Monroe, Gray's uncle. He's the voice you heard on Gray's phone yesterday. If you're certain that's the guy who shot you, then that's who has Lili," he grits out.

I follow Alessandro back inside the building as he reaches into his waistband and draws a pistol. Why the fuck don't I carry? That's something I can rectify later. Right now, I want to burn this place to the goddamn ground.

Alessandro slams through a door and then he's pointing his gun right at Grayson's head. "Where the fuck is my sister?"

"I don't know, man." Gray holds his hands in the air. "We're running through the tapes now."

"Where the fuck is that uncle of yours?"

"Lou?" Gray's brows knit together.

"You got any others? Where the fuck is he?" Alessandro hisses.

"He's in Toronto."

"No, he's not. He's here. What's he want with my sister?" Alessandro is firing off question after question, his arm outstretched and that pistol aimed directly at Gray.

"I've got no fucking idea, but if he's done something to her, I'll fucking kill him myself," Gray says between gritted teeth.

Aurora's gasp has me looking in her direction and then up at the wall-mounted screen she's staring at. Lili is being carried out of the arena. Her head lulls to the side.

"She's fucking unconscious," I growl. "Where the fuck is this guy?"

Grayson picks up his phone and makes a call. "Pops, where's Lou?" he asks. I don't hear his father's reply, but Gray nods. "Okay," he says as he sets the receiver down and looks to Alessandro. "Both of our fathers are almost here."

"Pull up the footage from the parking lot." Alessandro waves his gun towards the screen.

"You can put that thing down, you know. I'm not your enemy here," Gray tells him while tapping away on the keyboard.

"Right now, everyone is my fucking enemy," Alessandro counters.

I can't stop staring at the screen. We're all just standing around while Lili is unconscious and in the hands of a fucking lunatic. I don't look away. Not when a shit-ton of men enter the room. Not when I hear her father yelling out commands and throwing shit around. Not even when I feel someone's hand land on my shoulder. My eyes are glued to the stilled image of her being carried away. I pull my phone out of my pocket and dial her number. I don't know why I haven't tried it before now.

The call connects and I put it on speaker. "You really don't know how to take a fucking hint, do you, kid?" That voice... it's the same one I heard right before I was shot.

"Where the fuck is Liliana?" I growl.

"She's where she belongs. With me. Don't worry, you'll see her again. But it'll be too late by then. She'll be mine in every way possible."

I look to Mr. Valentino. His jaw is set tight, his

glare hyperfocused as he listens in while tapping at his phone. "Keep him talking," one of Lili's uncles whispers into my ear.

"She'll never be yours and we both know that. I'm going to fucking tear you limb from limb when I find you. I can't wait to watch you fucking bleed," I grunt.

"Those are big words from a no-good hockey player." The asshole laughs. "Give it your best shot, boy. You ain't got nothing I'm afraid of."

"Tell me where you are and I'll gladly show you firsthand," I hiss.

Mr. Valentino looks up from his phone. "You might not be afraid of him, Lou. But mark my words... when I get my hands on you, you're going to beg for fucking mercy. And I promise you, you won't get it," he says in an eerily calm voice.

The phone disconnects. My fingers clench around it.

Mr. Valentino glances at my hands before looking back up at me. "We got it. Let's go."

Chapter Thirty-Five

I bring my hand up to my head and rub, in an attempt to ease the throbbing. It doesn't work. Was I drinking? What the hell did I do to deserve this kind of torture?

I rack my brain, trying to figure out what I did.

The last thing I can remember is being at the arena, having made the decision to go and talk to Travis.

My eyes squeeze shut before I slowly open them, only to regret it immediately when the blinding light hits me.

"Argh, god!" I groan, roll over, and look towards the door. Except it's not there. I stare at the blank wall as I push myself up.

Where the hell am I?

My blurry vision begins to focus on things. Things I don't recognize. Like the white marble dresser that has nothing sitting atop of it. Or the single pink bedroom chair tucked into the corner of the room. I climb off the bed, my body aching with each step I make towards the door, which is not where I remember it being in the rental house.

My palm wraps around the handle. I turn it slowly and pull. Nothing happens. The door doesn't budge. I tug harder, and then harder again. What the fuck? My heart is racing in my chest as I take a step back and spin around. There has to be another way out of here. I cannot be locked inside this room. I can't be.

When I spot a second door, I grab the knob and turn, sending up a little prayer when it pushes open.

I curse under my breath when I realize it's a bathroom.

Shit. Think, Lili. Think, damn it.

What is it that Dad always says?

We were trained for situations like this. And yet, as the panic sets in, as my heart continues to race and sweat coats my forehead, I can't for the life of me remember what I'm supposed to do. I know what I *need* to do. And that's get out of this room. I look around the bathroom and step over to the window. It's older, the kind you should be able to slide up and down, but there's no movement no matter how much I try to push it open.

I pivot back towards the bedroom, shove the sheer curtains out of the way, and try each of the windows there. They're locked and there's no key in sight. When I peer through the glass, I don't see anything except for trees and more trees. Like I was dropped in the middle of the woods somewhere.

Where the fuck am I?

I suck in a steadying breath as I sink to my knees on the carpet. I just need to calm down and think.

Find a weapon, anything you can use to inflict damage.

My father's words flit through my mind. I need

to find something I can use to protect myself. There has to be something, anything. I push to my feet and walk over to the dresser first, pulling open drawer after drawer. They're all empty. I try the bedside table next. I bend down and look under it while feeling around.

"Well, that would have been too fucking easy," I murmur to myself. We usually have a gun or knife secured to the underside of furniture like this at home. The sound of keys jingling has me straightening up and spinning around. The door opens, and I blink at the figure filling the doorway. "What's going on? Why am I here?"

"You're here because you were a very naughty girl, Liliana. You went and slutted yourself out to that hockey player when you were always meant to be mine," Lou Monroe sneers at me.

I shake my head. "I don't know what you're talking about, Lou. You need to let me out." I glance behind him. At the door.

"Oh, I will, once you learn your place. But right now, I have a surprise for you, sweetheart. I'll be right back. Don't you go anywhere." He laughs as he slams the door closed again.

I rush forward and try to open it, but it doesn't

budge. Shit. Gray's uncle? What the hell is happening? I've only met the man a couple of times. I've never even had a real conversation with him. I just need to stay calm. My father will be looking for me by now. He'll find me. And God help anyone who tries to get in his way.

I step back when the door is flung open for a second time and a different man walks in, his eyes wide and full of fear. Lou is behind him, pressing a pistol to the back of his head.

"Darling, meet Harry. He's a celebrant and has agreed to marry us," Lou says while nudging the guy farther into the room. Harry trips and lands on his hands and knees. "Get the fuck up, you weak bastard," Lou barks as spittle peppers the air.

I shake my head. This cannot be happening to me right now. "No, Lou, you need to let me go. If you stop this now, I can talk to my father. I can make sure he doesn't kill you."

Lou laughs. "You think I'm scared of your pathetic excuse for a father? No, we're getting married today, Liliana. Our families will be joined. *You and I* will be joined. And then I'll take over, rule that little empire of yours. It'll be mine."

I shake my head again. That's not how it works. That's not how any of it works. And I would think a man like Lou Monroe, a man who grew up in the life, would understand as much.

I don't say any of that, though. The guy is clearly off his rocker. And I don't want to aggravate the situation. My eyes drop to Harry, who is pulling himself up off the floor. He's an older gentleman with gray hair and light wrinkles on his face.

"Get the paperwork. Say whatever bullshit you gotta say and get this done. My bride and I have a busy night ahead of us," Lou says before winking at me.

My stomach twists. I swallow down the fear. Now is not the time to show fear. My attention remains hyperfocused on that gun. If I can just get it off him, I can end this. I'm not an idiot, though. Lou is a big guy. There's no way I can overpower him without some kind of leverage.

"Sign here." The celebrant's hands shake as he holds out a piece of paper and a pen for me to take.

"No. I'm not marrying Lou." My voice is firm, unwavering, as I swallow down my nerves.

"Sign the fucking papers, Liliana." Lou turns the gun on me.

"You're not going to shoot me. If you do, you lose everything. Everything you're looking to gain from my family," I tell him while hoping like hell that I'm right.

"You're right," he says, as if reading my mind. "I'm not going to shoot you. But him?" Lou swipes the barrel through the air and levels it at Harry. "He's nothing. I'll shoot him without a second thought. Do you want that kind of blood on your hands, Liliana?"

I look at the old man, who's very clearly innocent in all this. "No, I don't," I say.

"Then sign on the fucking dotted line." Lou snatches the paper and pen from Harry's hand and shoves them towards me.

It's just a bit of paper. It doesn't mean anything.

That's what I'm telling myself as I scrawl my name across the bottom of the page. I belong to Travis. Nothing Lou Monroe does to me will ever change that.

"You're now man and wife," the celebrant says as he stamps the documents at the bottom. The second the words are out of his mouth, the sound of gunfire blasts through my ears. Blood splatters across my face, and I blink a few times as I watch Harry's body topple forward and hit the ground with an audible thud.

"There's a robe in the bathroom. Clean yourself

up and put it on. I'll be back—oh, and smile, Liliana. It's our wedding night after all. And I plan to make the experience something you'll never forget." Lou turns around and walks out the door, leaving me standing here staring down at Harry's lifeless corpse, the old man's blood pooling around what's left of his head before seeping into the carpet.

Chapter Thirty-Six

As soon as the car comes to a stop, I jump out and run. I can hear my name being called, along with several expletives and a string of Italian I don't understand. But the sentiment is clear. No one is happy with me right now. I don't care. All I care about is finding her. Getting to her.

I push past the pain tearing through my body as I kick in the door. To my surprise, it caves in on the first try.

"Stop!" Mr. Valentino tugs me back by the collar of my shirt. He has a gun in each hand as he pushes past me and into the house.

I follow him, my gaze flicking around the derelict building. The house is quickly stormed by the rest of the Valentino men, each room coming up empty.

"She's not here. Where the fuck is she? She was supposed to be fucking here!" I throw a fist through the closest wall. I barely feel it when my knuckles embed in the drywall.

Enzo turns a corner and stalks my way with a phone in one hand and a gun in the other. "This is hers. Bastard planted it," he says.

"Alessandro, street cams. Pull up the footage. He's been in the area recently. I wanna know what he's driving. I want license plates and registration information," Mr. Valentino says.

I raise my fist and slam it into the wall for a second time. "Fuck."

With each minute that passes, my soul is dying a

kylie Kent

little more. Thoughts of what he could be doing to her plague my mind. My fist clenches again, and I pull my arm back. But before I can make contact with the wall, my arm is grabbed. I turn to see Lili's father.

"That's not going to help. Let's go," he grunts, dropping my arm and walking out of the house.

It might not help. But, fuck... I need to do something. I need to fucking find her. And all I can fucking do is follow her family around while hoping like fuck they live up to their namesake.

Please let her be okay. Please let us find her before it's too late. Please, God, do not take her from me. I can't do this life without her.

"We're going to find her," Enzo says from where he's positioned beside me in the car. I wish I could believe him. Take his words for gospel. But I can't.

"What if..." I can't even finish my sentence. *What if... we're too late?*

"Don't think about the *what ifs*. Liliana is strong. She's been trained for situations like this her whole life. She will be okay. She'll hold tight until we get there. Because she trusts that we will. She knows we will," he says.

I know she's strong. I know she's more than capable. But that doesn't mean she should be forced to prove it. To endure whatever he's doing to her right now.

We head back to the Valentino's rental property. I don't want to be here. I need to be out there doing something. I need to find her.

But where the fuck do I even start?

I follow Lili's father and brother into the office and pace back and forth as they pull up street cam footage on the large screens attached to the wall. My eyes scan every camera for any sign of her. I just need to get a glimpse. Anything that lets me know she's still breathing. That her heart is still beating.

I would know if it wasn't, though, wouldn't I?

I would feel it. Surely I would feel when the other half of my soul is gone.

I run my hands through my hair. I can't think like that. I'm going to find her. We're going to find her. We have to.

"There." Jacob Monroe points to one of the screens. "That's him," he says.

I close the distance and peer up at the footage.

The image isn't all that clear, but I see a man in a shitty old pickup truck.

"You sure?" Mr. Valentino asks.

"I know." Jacob Monroe nods.

I look at him. If it is Lou, the man is handing over his own brother. Sending him to his death. Because there is no doubt in my mind that the Valentinos are already planning what they're going to do to this fucker. They are not just going to let him walk away from this.

Then again, for all I know, Jacob could be sending them on a wild goose chase to give his brother more time to get away. My stomach drops. What if he's not even in the country anymore? These people have the means to disappear for good.

"I'm tracking the license plates now," Alessandro says while tapping away at a keyboard.

"I've got it," Lili's uncle—Romeo, I think—says as he points a remote to a different screen. "I'm following the car's movements."

I remain glued to the spot, watching each turn the car makes. There's nothing I can do but stand and wait for it to fucking stop. When it finally does, Romeo calls out an address and everyone runs out the door. There are at least ten SUVs blocking the street. I jump into the one with her father and brother. None of us says a word as the car takes off.

"Do not run in blind, Travis. Stay the fuck behind us," Mr. Valentino tells me when we hit the highway.

"I need to get her back," I say instead of agreeing with him.

"And we will get her back, but I'm not watching her fucking heart break all over again because you decided to be reckless and get yourself killed. Stay behind us. She needs you alive."

I nod, even though there's no way I'm staying behind. If she's in that house, I'm going to get to her and no one is going to fucking stop me from doing it.

Chapter Thirty-Seven

T his isn't happening. My ass hits the ground as my knees give out on me. I close my eyes, but when I open them again, I'm met with the same image. Harry's lifeless body.

How long have I been here? And where is my dad?

I've never doubted my father's ability to protect me. To keep me safe. To find me if I ever needed finding. I'm not going to start doubting him now. He's coming for me. I know he is. Guilt for even thinking that he put a hit out on Travis eats away at my subconscious. I should have known my dad wouldn't do anything that could hurt me.

It's not long before regret sinks in too. I've wasted the last week trying to keep Travis safe by staying away from him. He was hurt. He needed me. And I wasn't there. I should have been there. Staying away wasn't the answer. I get that now, and I'm afraid he will never know how sorry I am. How much I love him. I made him doubt my love. Even if it was that same love that had me willing to break us to save him.

Does he know that I've been taken? Is he looking for me? He's not accustomed to this kind of thing happening. Not that I am. But I have seen people disappear. Some of them are found. Most of them are not. I understand the reality of my situation, which is why I manage to creep closer to the old man's body. My hands fumble as I search his pockets. There has to be something...

"Please just have a pen, anything really." I look around the floor. There *was* a pen. I remember there being a pen to sign that bullshit marriage license. Where did it go?

I saw Lou take the piece of paper with him. But did he take the pen too? I can't recall.

I search the pockets inside Harry's jacket and pull out his wallet. Opening it, I'm met with a picture of a woman and two younger girls. My heart breaks for the strangers staring back at me. They've just lost someone important to them, and there wasn't a single thing I could do to stop it. I don't find anything else in his pockets. No phone. Nothing.

My hope of actually getting out of this unscathed is wavering. I know my dad is going to find me. I know that he and my uncles and my cousins... my brother... they're all looking for me. And I know just how ruthless they will be until they hunt us down. Part of me can't help but wonder if it will be too late, though...

I don't know how long I've been sitting here, next to Harry, when the door rattles again. I jump up and move to the other side of the room. Creating as much space between myself and Lou Monroe as I can. He walks in dressed in a bathrobe.

"Why aren't you cleaned up?" he yells and charges forward with only the bed standing between us now. "You're going to have to learn the hard way that when I tell you to do something, you're going to fucking do it or face the consequences."

I watch his movements, and as he rounds the bed, I jump up on the mattress and bolt to the other side. My aim is to get to the door. I just need to get to the door. I'm only a few more steps away when his hand reaches out, wraps around my ankle, and pulls me backwards.

"No!" I scream out as I frantically try to grip onto something. Anything. My body is flipped over, and his weathered palm comes down across my face so fast I don't have time to move or avoid the contact. A sharp sting burns my cheek.

"I told you to fucking clean yourself up. You think I want to fuck my wife when she's covered in the blood of some other man?" Another quick slap leaves my skin hot to the touch. "If you won't do it, I'll do it myself."

I can feel my body being lifted. I'm still dazed from the blows. My head turns to the side, and that's when I see the lamp. My arm reaches out, my fingers close around the base, and I bring it down on Lou's skull as hard as I can before lifting it and repeating the process.

His body slumps on top of me, nearly suffocating me with the full force of his weight. I drop the lamp and push at his shoulders before I finally manage to get out from under him. Lou slumps onto the floor. I don't stop to see if he's come to yet. Instead, I scoot across the bed and run. Out the door, down the stairs, and through a kitchen.

That's where I stop when my eyes land on the wooden block sitting on the counter. I pull out the knife with the biggest handle. I will not be helpless. I have no idea what makes me do it, but I find myself walking back up the stairs. And into the bedroom. Lou is still sprawled out on the floor. Seemingly unconscious. That doesn't stop me from falling to my knees beside him. I lift the knife above his chest, and with as much strength as I can muster, I bring it down. It takes a lot more force to stab someone than you would think. My hands tremble and my muscles ache.

"Fuck you, asshole," I scream as I lift the knife and stab him again. Over and over until my body is drained of energy. I have nothing left.

Then I drop the bloody knife to the floor and dig through Lou's pockets. I sigh when my fingers wrap around a phone. I tap on the screen and it lights up.

"Shit."

What the fuck is the password?

I can't even begin to guess so I pick up his limp

hand and press each of his fingertips to the button on the side, hoping one of them will unlock the screen. When I get to his pinky, I finally hit pay dirt.

"Who uses their pinky to open their phone?" I question aloud as I type in my dad's number.

"Hello?" His voice sounds strained. Tentative.

"Daddy," I sob with relief.

"Liliana, baby, where are you?"

"I... I don't know."

"Stop the fucking car," Dad yells to whoever's in the background before returning his focus to me. "Liliana, I need you to stay on the line. Are you... are you okay?"

"I'm okay. But I need you to come and get me," I tell him as tears run down my face.

"I'm coming. Just stay on the line," he repeats. Then he's talking to someone else again. "I have her on the phone. Find out where this call is coming from. Now." I hear some shuffling. "Liliana, Zio Romeo is pinning your location now."

"I'm sorry. I'm so sorry."

"This is not your fault, baby. Remember the flowers, Liliana. What was your favorite color rose again?" Dad asks me.

I look around the room. "Red," I tell him. The question is code, a way to let him know if there's anyone else with me. Red represents blood. It means I'm the only one here who's still breathing. It tells him I'm alone.

I can hear him sigh into the phone. "I love you, Liliana, and I'm coming for you."

"I love you too. I'm sorry I doubted you, Daddy. I'm so sorry."

"Zio Romeo has your location. We're ten minutes out. Do not hang up, baby."

"Dad, Travis... I..."

"He's right here, Lil. He's right next to me, and we're coming," Dad says.

Then I hear his voice. "Lili, I'm coming for you."

"I'm sorry." I'm a broken record, I know. But it seems to be the only thing I can say. "I love you, and I messed everything up. I know that. I... I was coming to see you. I wanted to tell you."

"Lili, you haven't messed anything up. I love you. I will always love you," Travis says.

I hear the screeching of tires.

"We're here, sweetheart," Dad says as the sounds of heavy footsteps echo through the house. I push to my feet and walk to the doorway right as Travis lands at the top of the stairs.

He rushes forward, his arms wrapping around me tighter than they ever have before. "Fuck," he curses as he pulls back to look me up and down. "Are you hurt? What the fuck did that bastard do to you?"

"Nothing. It's... it's not my blood," I tell him as my dad and brother push through the bedroom door with their nines raised. Then I hear the gunshots, one after another. When I peer back inside the room, I see my father standing over Lou's body.

He returns his nine to its holster, walks over to me, and cups my face in his hands. "I'm sorry it took so long," he says.

"It's okay. I knew you would find me." I give him a small smile, and he presses his lips to my forehead.

"Let's get you home, sweetheart."

The whole time my father is talking to me, Travis is here too. His grip tight as he stands as close to me as he can get. He bends at the waist and picks me up.

"No, put me down. You can't carry me!"

"The hell I can't," he grunts as we descend the stairs.

"Travis O'Neil, you're going to pop a stitch!" I tell him.

Chapter Thirty-Eight

Ignoring everyone else, I carry Lili into the house. Our house. Our home. I didn't realize her father told the driver to take us here until we were pulling up. This is not how I pictured this going. Lili finally seeing our place for the first time.

But she's here now, and I'm not fucking letting her go.

As we're walking up the stairs, I can't help but hear her father tell Alessandro not to follow us. I don't look back, though. I continue straight into our bedroom and close the door.

I don't set her down again until I carry her into the bathroom. I reach in the shower stall and turn on the water before I pull my shirt over my head and drop it to the floor. I grab for Lili's sweater next. She lifts her arms and helps me tug it off her. Neither one of us says a word as we strip down. Taking her hand, I lead her under the spray and pull her body against mine. Red tints the droplets and pools around our feet.

"I love you so fucking much," I whisper into her neck. "I was so fucking scared."

"I'm sorry," she says. "I love you, Travis. I shouldn't have pushed you away like I did."

"No, you shouldn't have. But I also shouldn't have let you. I should have fought harder," I admit. "Never again, Lili. I'm not going to be apart from you ever again."

I let go of her so I can reach behind her head and pick up the loofah. I squirt some bodywash on it before lifting her left arm and running the loofah over her skin, repeating the process until the water is clear again.

Lili sucks in a huge breath. "Mmm, I like smelling like you."

"I like you smelling like me too," I tell her, pausing before asking her what I really want to know. "Lili, did he...?" I can't even say the word.

"No." She shakes her head. "No, Travis, he didn't."

I cup her face. There are bruises forming on her right cheek, and my fingers tremble with rage.

"I'm okay," she says.

"I... I'm so fucking proud of you, Liliana."

"For what?" she asks as her eyebrows draw down.

"For how strong you are, how resilient you are. You saved yourself, babe. You didn't need anyone to save you. You did that all on your own. And that strength is something to admire." I kiss the middle of her forehead and her body leans into my touch.

"I killed someone, Travis. I killed Gray's uncle. I should feel something, right? I took a life." Lili's hands start shaking, and despite the warmth of the water, I can feel goose bumps rising all over her skin.

"No, you survived, babe."

"No, I ran. He was unconscious and I ran out of

the room. But then I went back up there when I saw the knife. And I stabbed him, over and over, until I couldn't stab him anymore. He wasn't even conscious and I kept going," she says.

"You did what you had to do. That's all."

"Maybe..."

"No fucking *maybes* about it." I tip her chin up and force her to look at me. I want her to see what I see when I look at her. How in awe I am.

Once we're both clean, I turn off the water and grab a towel from the shelf. I pat Lili down before getting another towel and wrapping it around her. After I dry myself off, I take her hand and lead her out to the bedroom. I pull a shirt out of the closet and tug it over her head as the towel drops from her body.

"Do you want to go downstairs?" I ask as I pull a pair of sweats up my legs.

Lili shakes her head and her eyes flick to the bed. "Not yet. I just want to lie down."

I take her hand in mine again, lead her over to the bed, and pull the blankets back. I climb in after her, covering us both up before pulling her into my arms. "How long do you think they'll leave us alone in here?"

"Not long," she says with a yawn. "I'm so tired."

"Go to sleep, babe. I've got you," I tell her.

I lie still while holding the girl who has become my whole fucking world in my arms. I watch as her body relaxes and she drifts off to sleep. I don't move an inch, not wanting to disturb her.

My head turns to the door when it opens a few minutes later, and I bring a finger to my lips, telling her father and brother to be quiet. Their eyes drop to Lili before landing on me again.

"How is she?" her father asks, keeping his voice low.

"She's okay."

He nods, and it looks like he wants to say something else. I also get the feeling he wants nothing more than to reach into this bed and drag his daughter out of it. He doesn't, though, which I'm grateful for. Because he'd have to pry her from my cold, dead hands. And there's been enough bloodshed around my girl today.

"My men found a marriage certificate at the house. That bastard forced her to sign it," Mr. Valentino says after a long pause.

"He what?" I ask through gritted teeth, a new bout of rage boiling beneath my surface.

"It's not legally binding, but she wouldn't have known that," he says. "Let me know when she wakes up." He turns and walks towards the door. Stopping before he leaves the room to glance back at me over one shoulder. "Travis, don't fuck this up."

I nod my head at him. I'm guessing that's as good as an approval I'll ever get from the man. Well, that and the fact that he's not actively trying to get rid of me or threatening to kill me anymore.

Alessandro lingers at the end of the bed for another minute before he follows his father out of the room.

"I will never fuck this up," I whisper my promise to Lili. "I love you."

She stirs in my arms, and I tighten my hold on her. I don't dare fall asleep, though. Instead, I watch her while I plan out the rest of our lives.

A few hours later, Lili blinks her eyes open. "Travis?" she questions.

"Yeah, babe, I'm here," I tell her as I lean over and kiss her temple.

Lili rolls over onto her back. "Kiss me properly."

"With fucking pleasure." I turn onto my side, grip her chin in my fingers, and gently press my lips to hers.

Lili takes hold of the back of my head, tugging me harder against her as she pushes her tongue into my mouth. Deepening the kiss. This right here, with her, feels like heaven.

I pull back to look at her. "Promise me that you're never leaving again."

"I promise," she says. "I will never leave. You are my heart and soul, Travis O'Neil."

"And you are my everything, Liliana Valentino. I refuse to lose you again."

Lili smiles at me. "You never lost me. I was always yours."

I press my lips to hers again as I slip my tongue back into her mouth and hear her soft moans. I close my eyes and see that familiar shade of red. This woman lights up my world. She is my end goal.

Epilogue

Liliana

Three months later

"Who's that girl?" I ask Kathryn while nodding at the blonde currently walking in next to Luke Jameson, Travis's teammate and new friend. I swear Luke,

Gray, and Liam are at our house more often than not these days.

"That's Montana. She's the little sister of Luke's childhood best friend," Aliyah chimes in. "She just got into town and is staying at his place."

I turn to Aliyah and laugh. "How is it that you always seem to know everything about everyone?"

I've known the girl my whole life, but over the past three months, I've gotten to know her a lot better and she's become one of my best friends.

"It helps to be the owner's daughter." She shrugs. "Also, Liam is the biggest gossip around. That man cannot keep a secret if his life depends on it." She laughs.

"Good to know. Remind me not to divulge anything to him then." I bump shoulders with Kathryn.

Kathryn and Gray's six-year-old daughter is bouncing up and down. Her eyes fixated on the ice and her little hands sprawled out on the glass in front of us. "It's going to start soon," Graycee says.

The game is set to begin in ten minutes, which is why Luke walking into the suite with this woman right now has us all so curious.

"Aliyah, this is Montana. Montana, Aliyah." Luke waves a hand between the pair. "And this is

Kathryn and Liliana," he adds, gesturing to Kathryn and then me. "Montana's going to watch the game up here with you all."

"Great, come on. Let me get you a drink." Aliyah hooks her arm around Montana's and leads her away from Luke. I notice how he watches her for a bit before landing his glare on us again. It looks like he wants to say something but then he just turns and walks out of the room.

"You felt that weird vibe too, right?" I ask, keeping my voice low enough so that only Kathryn can hear me.

"Yep." She nods her head. "Come on, let's get the good seats," she says before tugging me back towards the window.

I don't bother telling her that they're all good seats. We're in the owner's box after all.

This is Travis's first game since the incident. He's been waiting for this moment for months now. His first official game as a Knight. Both of our parents are here to watch him too.

My mom walks over to me, concern knitting her brows. "You okay?"

"Uh-uh, just nervous. I want everything to go well for him," I say.

"It will. I have a feeling today is going to be an

343

unforgettable day for the both of you." She smiles at me.

"What do you mean?"

"Nothing. I need to go and stop your father from drinking the bar dry." She walks off, and I follow her movements as she makes her way over to where Dad is leaning against the back wall. He doesn't even have a drink in his hand.

The lights go down, and I return my attention to the window. I pull my phone from my pocket and hold it up, ready to snap a picture the moment Travis's skates hit the ice.

Epilogue

I look up. There're only two minutes left on the clock. And we're up by three. One of which is thanks to yours truly. The feeling of being back out here, playing the game, hearing the fans scream my name... it's euphoric. Knowing that Lili is watching makes it ten times better.

345

I look over to the bench where she's seated. I asked her parents to make sure she was down here before the end of the game. They know what I'm planning. I didn't exactly get her father's permission but I respect the guy enough to not blindside him either.

Especially after the incident with Lou Monroe and the forced marriage license. It took Liliana a while to recover from that bullshit. She was terrified the whole thing was real, afraid that Lou had sent the paperwork off before she'd stopped him. Her father assured her that none of it was legal and held on to the certificate so Lili could burn it herself.

When the final buzzer sounds out, the whole arena lets out a roar. I wait for everyone to leave the ice before I skate over to the bench where Liliana is clapping and smiling so damn hard. I wrap my arms around her waist and pick her up, carrying her out to the middle of the rink as the lights shine a bright red, with a single spotlight on us.

"What's going on?" Liliana asks as she looks around.

Everyone in the stands is on their feet as I drop to a knee. And Lili gasps, bringing a hand to her mouth. Reaching inside my jersey, I tug out the chain on my neck and hold up the diamond ring.

"Liliana Valentino, you are more than I ever could have asked for, more than I'll ever deserve. I promise to love you, to put you above everything else. To always support you in whatever you choose to do throughout our lives. Will you let me give you my last name? Will you marry me?" I ask her.

Lili collapses to her knees in front of me, and I know hitting the ice like that's gotta hurt. She doesn't even flinch, though. "Yes." Her arms fly out and wrap around my neck, knocking me onto my back. "Yes, yes, yes!" she repeats as her lips crash onto mine.

The horns blast through the arena and the crowd whistles and yells out their congratulations.

"Lili, babe, as much as I want to fuck you right now with nothing but this ring on, we're in the middle of the ice," I remind her.

Lili pushes off me, sits up, and holds out her left hand. "You forgot the part where you put that ring on my finger, Travis."

"I didn't forget. You body-checked me before I got the chance, babe." I slide the diamond into place and narrow my glare at her. "This never comes off."

"Never," she agrees.

Then I push to my skates and scoop her up. Lili's legs wrap around my waist, and those red lips press against mine as I carry her back over to the bench. Determined to never let her go again.

**Are you curious to see what's going on
with Luke and Montana?
Follow the Vancouver Knights' journey
with the final installment in the series:
Puck Blocked.**

Club Omerta

Are you a part of the Club?

Don't want to wait for the next book to be released to the public?
Come and Club Omerta for an all access pass!

This includes:
- daily chapter reveals,
- first to see - everything, covers, teasers, blurbs
- Advanced reader copies of every book
- Bonus scenes from the characters you love!
- Video chats with me (Kylie Kent)
- and so much more

Click the link to be inducted to the club!!!
CLUB OMERTA

About the Author

About Kylie Kent

Kylie made the leap from kindergarten teacher to romance author, living out her dream to deliver sexy, always and forever romances. She loves a happily ever after story with tons of built-in steam.

She currently resides in Sydney, Australia and when she is not dreaming up the latest romance, she can be found spending time with her three children and her husband of twenty years, her very own real life instant-love.

Kylie loves to hear from her readers; you can reach her at: author.kylie.kent@gmail.com

Let's stay in touch, come and hang out in my readers group on Facebook, and follow me on instagram.

Made in the USA
Columbia, SC
04 August 2024

39981747R00196